*Working Women
and
Other Stories*

Working Women and other stories

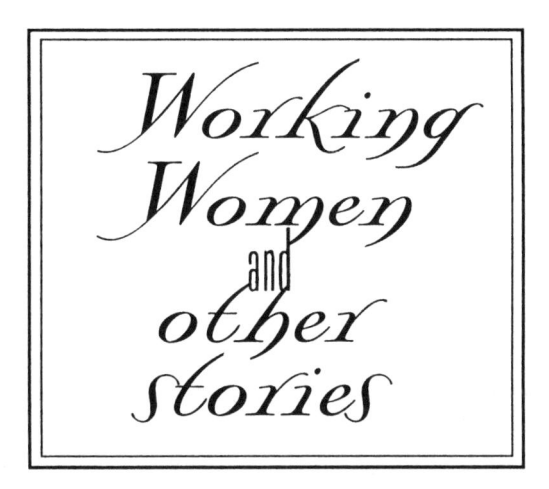

TRICIA BAUER

Bridge Works Publishing Co.
Bridgehampton, New York

Copyright © Tricia Bauer

All rights reserved under International and
Pan-American Copyright Conventions.

Published in 1995 in the United States by Bridge Works Publishing Co.,
Bridgehampton, New York.
Distributed in the United States by National Book Network,
Lanham, Maryland.

First Edition

The characters and events in this book are fictitious. Any similarity to actual persons, living or dead, is coincidental and not intended by the author.

The following stories originally appeared, in slightly different form, in the publications listed: "Pot o' Gold" in *Black Warrior Review*: "Dancing with the Movies" in *American Literary Review*; "Panama" in *Fiction Network*; "Beds" in *The Massachusetts Review*; "Fortunes" in *First* (as "In the Cards"); "Dogs" in *Hawaii Pacific Review*; "Visiting Hours" in *The American Voice*; "Sauna" in *Kalliope*; "Gypsies" in *Indiana Review*; "The Graveyard" in *Carolina Quarterly*.

Library of Congress Cataloging-in-Publication Data

Bauer, Tricia
  Working women and other stories / Tricia Bauer.—1st ed.
   p. , cm.
   ISBN 1-882593-11-1 (hard cover : alk. paper)
   1. United States—Social life and customs—1971- —Fiction.
I. Title.
PS3552.A83647W67   1995
813'.54—dc20   95-14083
                                                         CIP

10 9 8 7 6 5 4 3 2 1

Book and jacket design by Eva Auchincloss
Printed in the United States of America

for Bozzone

Contents

Pot o' Gold	1
Dancing with the Movies	23
Panama	45
Beds	53
Fortunes	65
Dogs	81
Visiting Hours	95
Sign	103
Working Women	113
Sauna	129
Gypsies	141
The Blue Room	155
The Graveyard	173
Nocturne	189

*Working Women
and
Other Stories*

Pot o' Gold

I wasn't even going to take the job, but Evan convinced me to give it a shot. Evan and I met in college. He had graduated the year before me, and now worked as an investigative reporter for the Richmond *Times-Dispatch*. "Think like a reporter," he said. "Even in the smallest places, there's room for a story."

It was the summer I'd quit school to stop taking sides in my parents' arguments. Two semesters away from a degree in journalism, I could have opted to stay in Hillsdale, Virginia, with my tearful mother and continue receiving a state scholarship, or drive with my father to Florida in his red VW van and attend the college of my choice. Or so he promised.

Instead, I moved in with Evan and went on the first job interview that I got a call for. A soft male voice on the other end of the line divulged that Box C45—one of the many blind box ads for "assistant" that I'd mailed my résumé to—belonged to *Pot o' Gold* magazine. Before dressing for the interview, I left a note in case Evan stopped home for lunch.

The magazine's office was located over Limber's Hardware, well off the main street of town. At the end of a long hallway painted the pea green of old public swimming pools, I found the sign for *Pot o' Gold*. When I opened the door, the sounds of tapping, typing, and paper fluttering stopped completely. Deep inside the room, the boss sat behind a huge, highly polished desk while women spread out around him in a protective formation like worker bees guarding the queen. He gestured for me to approach and then, in a voice stripped of the politeness I'd detected over the phone, yelled, "Back to work, ladies."

Chester Trumble was at least sixty and wore thick black-framed glasses, which he continually rescued from the tip of his nose. He moved slowly and carefully, permitting his greasy hair, combed forward from the back of his head to disguise his receding hairline, to rest undisturbed. When he hunched forward to talk to me, I prepared myself for hot, bad breath. Instead, a surprisingly light, minty scent surrounded his words. The job interview consisted of a few comments, which I strained to hear over the office machines around me, and a typing test. As instructed, I set up and copied a business letter to myself:

> Dear Friend:
>
> Congratulations! You are a winner in this month's World Scrambler contest. Now it's time for more fun. Due to the many qualified entries we received, we have devised a tiebreaker contest. Please complete the enclosed puzzle and return it along with one dollar to POT o' GOLD magazine by June 15. And good luck.
>
> > Yours sincerly,
> > Chester Trumble
> > President and Director, Pot o' Gold

"You sounded good," said Chester as I handed him the letter. "Your typing," he clarified, not noticing I'd misspelled "sincerely." Chester promptly led me into the hall and shook my hand. Then he pulled at his ear and told me all talk of salary should be kept strictly confidential. "Welcome aboard," he said. "I'll see you tomorrow then."

That night Evan and I had a fight. I said I didn't want to work for a man who combed his hair with such obvious deception. Also, my instincts told me a one-room operation over Limber's Hardware would not improve my résumé. Evan took neither of these arguments seriously. He was uncompromising, at times even self-righteous, about his career. Having lived with him less than a month, I already saw how his mission to unearth an important story made him immune to personal agendas. Stepping in and out of emotionally charged incidents as skillfully as a performer dipping a baton of flame down his throat was Evan's idea of being a good reporter.

When I explained that the magazine was filled not with thoughtful feature stories but with a variety of word contests, which apparently required only an entry fee and a grade-school education, Evan nodded. He said I should at least try the job for a couple of weeks. He was not the kind of guy to throw anything away without careful consideration, not the plastic dishes from microwave dinners, not the possibility of a story idea for the *Times-Dispatch*. The letter I had copied for my typing test fascinated him, and he advised me to sniff around for anything unusual. He was looking for story angles.

"I do need the money," I said finally. I was thinking not only of helping Evan with the rent, but also of saving for my senior year tuition.

"Money's not the point, Dara," he yelled from behind the bedroom door. But then I saw money as a means to maintain balance. If I received my own salary, I would not have to choose the support of one of my parents over the other. Money, too, would keep Evan and me on equal terms. He might have a degree in journalism, but he didn't make what I had been offered, especially if you considered all his uncompensated overtime.

Evan liked to end disagreements quickly, but he never let them go completely. So even as he pulled me into the bedroom with him, as we took off each other's clothes and rocked ourselves away to a forgiving place, I knew he would remember all that I'd said during that argument.

My first day of work, Chester asked me to help Martha, a nervous young woman with a crop of curls that hid much of her face. With an X-acto knife, she sliced waxed lines and tiny numbers and stuck them into the formation of an unconventional crossword puzzle. The next step involved placing a letter in all but one of the squares for each word. I read the clue that went to 3 down: "A __ shake could sometimes be good for a child." The possible answers from a list of words were "mild" and "milk." Another clue read, "You might have this in summer." Answer choices were "tan" and "fan."

"What about 'man'?" I wondered aloud to Martha. She didn't crack a smile. I tried again. "Does anybody ever win these things?" I asked her, after reading the disclaimer stating that the words listed were only suggestions. I thought I'd spoken quietly, but Chester looked up at me over his glasses.

"Oh, eventually," Martha said, shrugging her shoulders.

"Back to work, Martha," Chester admonished. He tugged his ear, and Martha lowered her head at the same time, as if some invisible thread connected them. I looked around and noticed then that all actions going on in the room appeared somehow connected; each simple gesture started or contributed to a chain reaction. I felt that even I was a part of this system as one or another of the women in the room glanced up from her work to check on me. I kept my mouth shut until lunchtime.

At exactly noon, Martha and I, along with Joan, Sally Ann, and two deaf sisters, Ellen and Helen, filed behind a partition at the back of the room. Chester's desk was located just in front of this divider. As the women pulled their lunch bags from a tiny refrigerator, I asked, "Is it always this quiet around here, or did somebody just die?" It was the kind of comment that Evan would have gotten a kick from. The way these women stared at me, I feared that somebody *had* died, that I was, perhaps, the replacement for a woman who had shared recipes and lunches and stories with them. My face must have gone white, because Joan assured me I hadn't said anything offensive. She rolled her eyes and pointed at the partition that didn't quite reach the ceiling; everything we said could be heard by Chester.

Ellen and Helen proceeded to exchange fruit and sandwich halves in an elaborate, wordless ritual. "This goes on every day," Joan said, nodding to the sisters. "You'll get used to it." She turned from me and asked Martha, "How was the fitting?"

Martha smiled a broad smile, the ends of it concealed in her curly hair. She described her future wedding dress down to the number of pearls sewn into the bodice.

"I swear, after we finish paying for everything, we're not going to have the money to do anything but stay home and watch TV," said Martha, without seeming depressed.

"Welcome to the club," said Joan, who'd been married twenty-one years. "We joined this health and fitness deal, you know? And Dan—" Joan stopped and said directly to me, "Dan's my husband." She turned back to the group. "Dan says we can take showers at the clubhouse and that will keep our hot water bills down at home."

"That's goin' too far if you ask me," said Sally Ann. Sally Ann had a strong southern accent and arm muscles like I'd never seen on a woman.

"Who asked you?" said Joan, balling up her lunch bag.

Sally Ann excused herself to go to the ladies' room. As soon as she was gone Martha said, "She didn't mean nothin' by it. She's just upset is all."

Martha ignored me while Joan explained that Sally Ann's husband had run out on her and that their fifteen-year-old daughter was "giving her a fit." Joan said, "One day last week Sally Ann left work early because of a terrible headache. She got home and found her daughter horizontal on the sofa with a boy from the 7-11. Sally Ann about keeled over."

A sudden tapping on the partition disrupted the story and sent everyone hustling back to their work stations.

Martha didn't say a thing to me for the rest of the day. I watched her slide sheets of numbers and letters through a waxer and then cut the parts she needed for the puzzles. I whispered a question: Did she ever check the answers? She shook her head no and gestured in Chester's direction, meaning either that he went over the answers or that if she spoke to me she'd be reprimanded. I wanted to ask her if the woman whose place I'd taken had been a good friend, if that woman had been fired or had left for something better. I thought the woman must have something to do with the way Martha was ignoring me. Martha just kept her head down and didn't even look up when I sneezed.

The following day I was assigned to assist Sally Ann inputting contest entries and new subscribers' addresses into the computer. She didn't so much as say good morning, even after I slipped her a stick of Trident when Chester wasn't looking. At lunchtime, when Sally Ann still didn't speak to me, I knew something was peculiar at *Pot o' Gold*. Martha began to describe the decorations and flowers and cake she wanted for her wedding. Sally Ann said, "Just don't have birds. I read about this couple who planned for a bunch of doves to be released right after the vows were said."

"I think I heard this story somewhere," Joan interrupted.

Sally Ann said, "Let me finish. It was a really hot day and the doves were between the ceiling and the canopy. When the little flower girl pulled the cord to the canopy, a pack of dead birds dropped down all over the guests. Can you imagine?"

"That's disgusting," said Martha, putting her hands to her face.

When I wondered aloud if the couple was still married after having such a disaster at their wedding, Sally Ann looked away. Before I got another word out, there came the parental tapping from the other side of the partition.

I waited until Chester left the room. He ate at the corner deli at exactly 1:15 each day and was back in the office at 1:35. "I'll bet he eats the same thing every day, too," Joan had said the day before. By confiding his routine, she was telling me that only during those twenty minutes were we able to make or accept phone calls. She also advised me that I was to keep calls brief so everyone could have a turn.

"Will someone please tell me what's going on around here?" I asked as soon as Chester was out of the room. The room was as silent as if Chester were still behind his glossy desk. "Well, then, will you at least tell me about the person I replaced? Did you like her or hate her or did she die or what?"

Five women stared at me. Although the sisters were deaf,

even they appeared to know what was going on. If they didn't read lips, they shared an eerie extra sense that made even complex situations understandable.

Finally Joan spoke up. "You didn't replace anybody."

"What do you mean?" I asked.

"Just what I said. We figure the old man hired you to—what do they call it?" She looked around the room, then her eyes focused on the phone as if willing it to ring and deliver her from the awkward situation.

"Troubleshooting," said Sally Ann. I knew immediately that the group had had secret discussions about me, maybe on the way to their cars after work, maybe on the phone at night. I tried to explain that I was in the dark as much as they were about my job. I told them, and I believed this, that troubleshooting was a job I never would have accepted. I hadn't even thought of the possibility that "assistant" could imply deceit.

"Maybe I'm going to be a floater," I said, noticing that, unlike yesterday, nobody was making a beeline to the phone.

"A what?" asked Martha.

"You know. Somebody who goes from job to job, wherever they're needed." The deaf sisters were staring warily.

Joan sized me up for a long while. The only one who had been somewhat accepting of me, she finally said, "Well, I guess we can't complain about somebody who's going to give us a hand, can we, girls?" She didn't wait for an answer, just hollered, "Stomp on it. Here he comes." We'd all lost track of the time and Chester was rounding the corner outside. Suddenly I felt very young, part of a conspiracy against a teacher or parent that culminated in silence the moment the door opened.

Sally Ann and I sat down quickly at the computer. Before Chester made it to his desk, Sally Ann told me that she hadn't called home to check on her daughter, Kimberly. I decided that, trust me or not, she needed to voice her concern to someone: "I just wish that girl would listen to me and go off to college. Forget about these boys that will do nothin' but break your heart."

The walk home that night was incredibly hot. I'd lived through twenty-one Virginia summers, but never one with such uninterrupted intensity. The sidewalk held so much heat that I imagined it softening beneath me into a kind of clay. Somewhere in the world people were walking home in stinging cold with snow cracking beneath their feet. The thought of that far-off icy place comforted me all the way home.

By the time I reached the third floor of the building Evan and I lived in, my cotton blouse had soaked into me like another layer of skin. Without saying a word, Evan sat me in front of a small fan and went into the bathroom. In the time that we'd lived together, I'd learned not to crowd him with irrelevant talk when he was busy thinking about a story.

The fan's breeze was the temperature of Evan's breath. Hot. I looked around the room at his belongings. The mismatched furniture and too-short curtains. Some, of course, like the typewriter and gooseneck lamp, I remembered from school. I saw nothing to remind me that I lived here too, probably because I'd brought only one medium-size suitcase with me, filled mostly with clothes.

"I've got just the thing for you," said Evan, coming into the room. His voice startled me. Just when I'd figured out how to react to him, he'd do or say something out of character. He started to unbutton my blouse while leading me down the hallway toward the bathroom. The big, white, claw-footed tub was filled with cold water. He helped me out of the rest of my clothes and urged me into the tub. Once I was in all the way and had adjusted my body to the shock, Evan handed me a Budweiser. "There you go," he said.

The bathroom was the nicest room in Evan's apartment. The other rooms had been paneled to cover cracking plaster walls, and ceilings had been lowered, concealing the extravagant heights of the past. Only the bathroom retained its original character. Floor tiles the size of Scrabble pieces were arranged into mosaic designs. When I put my head back, I could watch the waning summer light filter through the pastels of an old skylight onto the cold water and onto me.

Heat that had been trapped in my body all day oozed into the water. The dark beer bottle sweated against my hand. I was relieved to be cooling off and happy to be with a considerate man.

Evan asked about *Pot o' Gold*. I took a swig of beer.

"I don't think they trust me. They haven't asked me about myself yet."

"What's not to trust?" Evan wriggled his fingers in the water.

I told him how Martha was afraid that she didn't work fast enough, how Sally Ann was concerned that Chester would warn her to leave her personal problems at home. "I think they're worried I'm supposed to replace one of them," I said finally.

"Are you?"

"I don't know." Then I acted out the lunch routine and got Evan laughing. Next I told him about Joan's grow-by-number garden, a kit of seed packets that, if planted according to a numerically outlined pattern, would grow into a famous painting.

"I told you I was skeptical of the place," I said smiling.

Gently he pushed me under water. It was delicious. When I came up, he was looking directly at me.

"Evan," I said, "I want those people to accept me."

"Who wouldn't accept you?" he asked sincerely, bending over me with one hand on either side of the tub.

"People who are different, who maybe don't have what I have." I was purposely being vague; I didn't know how to tell him that my own education, even though uncompleted, embarrassed me at *Pot o' Gold*.

"So tell them a story."

"Lie?"

"It's not really lying. Just don't tell them everything. People want to be with people who reinforce their lifestyles, their beliefs. Would you live with me if I were, say, a taxidermist?"

"Would you still make me a cold tub?"

He grinned and held open the towel with his fingertips. Those fingers that woke me up nights—either with their typing or their urgent groping for me.

—⋈—

The next day Chester assigned me to Joan's station—a large, cream-colored Formica table where she slit open the day's mail. As she worked I thought of my mother, who saved a stack of unopened bills until my father told her it was OK to pay them. Then, a sigh at the ready, she carefully opened each one, wrote the appropriate check, addressed the envelope, and affixed a stamp.

Joan held her sighs back that same way as she sorted through checks, cash, contest entry blanks, and letters. After checking each entry fee for accuracy, I added it to either the check pile or the cash pile, which Joan tallied on the adding machine every so often. The cash pile, outdistancing the check pile, grew higher than the telephone and halfway up the side of the lamp before Joan rang it up, recorded a figure, and we started again. I saw an entire Social Security check endorsed to *Pot o' Gold*. Now and then, I read one of the pieces of correspondence. A few of the letters were "punched up" by Chester and published in each issue of the magazine, but the majority of the generally handwritten pages were ripped up and thrown away.

> Dear Pot o' Gold:
>
> I haven't won anything yet, but maybe some day I will. I love word building puzzles. I've worked the puzzles for three years and I know I'll win soon. The part I especially like is you give a reasonable time to return the entries which makes it good for Senior Citizens. Have a nice day.
>
> Your loyal contestant,
> Mrs. Esther Jones
> Selma, Alabama

At lunchtime Joan asked me a question—the first—and the other women seemed to take her lead as an affirmation of confidence. "Where did you work before?" she asked as she unwrapped an olive loaf sandwich on rye bread.

Recalling Evan's advice, I answered immediately that I'd been a waitress in Hillsdale. My response wasn't totally false; as part of my scholarship at college I'd worked twenty hours a week in the school cafeteria. I didn't mention that I was two semesters away from a college degree. I didn't let on that I'd been to college at all.

Joan said she'd waitressed weekends in high school, but when she'd married Dan shortly after graduation, she had stopped working outside the home. Despite her ruddy complexion, I could see Joan blush as she talked about the early, sexy years of her marriage. I wondered if soon my own mother, who, like Joan, had never learned to type, would be forced to take a job where she reminisced about the days when her only worries were whether she could push me in the stroller to the grocery store and back before I cried for my next meal. I wondered if she would share with her coworkers the image of my father that still sat on the table next to the sofa. In the photo he was handsome and moustached and waved suggestively at the camera. Would she tell them, as she once revealed to me, how marriage had drained her of her self-reliance and left her empty and unlovable?

Joan said, loud enough for Chester to hear over the partition, that if it hadn't been for *Pot o' Gold* hiring her, she didn't know what she would have done.

Sally Ann, eating her tuna salad on a lettuce bed, said that she didn't like to think what would have happened to her and Kimberly if she hadn't gotten work after her husband left her. "My sister in Norfolk has been trying to reenter the job market for two years." Sally Ann's soft voice seemed out of keeping with her sharply defined face and strong arms, which were covered with long white-blonde hair that stood straight up when she was cold.

The deaf sisters stopped eating and looked at me as if I were the cause of this depressing conversation.

As soon as Martha got back from the bathroom she asked, "So, do *you* have a boyfriend?"

If I said I didn't, I knew they would try to fix me up on blind dates. And if I told them I had a boyfriend, they'd want to know when I was getting married. I made the leap; I told them I was married. Only after the words were out of my mouth did I wonder what Evan would think of this. Had I gone too far? We'd never mentioned the word in the context of our relationship.

"Where's your ring?" Martha asked quickly.

"What does he do?" Sally Ann asked at the same time.

I was not used to fabricating stories, but I came up with some pretty convincing answers: my ring was being sized smaller because I'd lost some weight since the wedding. "Jack" drove a truck for a local food distributor. I said I'd only been married three months, in the hope that that would stave off baby questions for the time being. I was surprised at how easy it was to tell people what they wanted to hear.

Evan had another cold bath waiting for me when I got home that evening. After a few swallows of beer, I told him that I must have seen three thousand dollars in cash while I was helping Joan open the mail. His eyes looked unnaturally green in the bright room.

"That's some operation," he said.

I shyly told him the part I'd made up about him and me.

"I told them your name was Jack."

Because Evan had never known me to lie, I couldn't tell what he was thinking. He put his hand into the water as if to test its temperature. All at once, he grabbed my wrist. "I knew it," he said. "I knew you were a reporter at heart."

"What?"

"Going under cover. This will be great. If you break this story, it could be big time."

"What story?"

"Come on, Dara. The no-win contest that sucks money from unsuspecting slobs."

"I don't know that yet," I said, surprised at Evan's attitude and shocked at the word "slobs." Evan didn't understand that I had lied to the women not to make some use of my situation at *Pot o' Gold*, but only to fit in.

When I stood up, Evan dabbed at the water running down me. Smiling proudly, he carried me into the bedroom and kissed me. When he said that good things were going to happen to me, I was unsure if he meant with "the story" or right then in bed.

On Friday I realized that *Pot o' Gold* did have at least a few winners. Printed at the top of my paycheck for the week was "Pot o' Gold Winners Club."

I'd spent all that day and the day before familiarizing myself with the work of the deaf sisters. Ellen gave me a lesson in eye-foot coordination when she showed me how to use the electric stapler. She slid the pages under the stapler, hit the foot pedal in rapid succession, and remained unmoved as I jumped at the gunlike sound. If I'd worked at that speed myself, I know my fingers could not have escaped a painful union with the pages of jumbles and puzzles and clues. Ellen also operated the huge postage machine at an incredible rate of speed.

The sisters were both overweight but otherwise didn't look much alike. Ellen had sharp features while Helen's were blunted. Helen's hair and skin were a shade darker than her sister's. If Ellen's forte was speed, Helen's was consistency. All day Helen folded and stuffed envelopes with subscription renewal requests and tiebreakers.

Chester was on his twenty-minute lunch and Martha was on the phone to her fiancé when I stopped folding and looked over one of the tiebreakers. This was the third tiebreaker in a contest for which entrants initially sent two dollars and unscrambled groups of letters to form "Ohio," "Maine," "Tennessee," and "New York." The tiebreaking lists of new jumbled words got progressively more difficult. The ten words on this entry were not ones I could easily decipher. There was no category clue either, as there had been with the "State Stakes." I asked around the room but no one seemed interested in the answers. Finally I figured out "deciduous." The other words I decided were medical terminology.

Sally Ann looked at me and said, "With that kind of mind you could go on television. You could clean up on one of the game shows."

I laughed, worried that she'd ask me why I hadn't gone to college. Instead, she picked up the phone just as Martha put it down, and called her daughter.

Chester took the computer home that weekend. Every Friday afternoon Ellen and Helen helped him carry the equipment to his dirty station wagon before they walked over to the bus stop. When I asked Joan what she thought Chester did on weekends, she told me she guessed he came up with the puzzle questions. She said this not without respect.

It wasn't long before I wondered whether, as Evan insisted, the entries for crosswords with answer choices such as "fan" and "tan" had been discovered *after* the puzzle was created. I supposed that all the contestants' responses were simply fed into the computer, and the least popular combination of answers became the winner.

For the next few weeks, I continued to rotate working among the women. All of us had begun to relax and accept my "floater" theory when Chester confused us by giving me a whole day to think of new names for word puzzles. He liked my suggestions of "Rich Pitch" and "Funny Money." Given the go-ahead to decorate the puzzle pages and liven up the cover for *Pot o' Gold*, I used clip art to design borders of leprechauns throwing dollar signs or coins into the air. I never portrayed anyone actually catching the money. But Chester didn't notice. Instead, he congratulated me in the long hallway that, in late afternoon, had taken on the color of soft, worn bills.

Each hot evening, I walked home ready for the respite I had looked forward to all day, Evan beside the cold bath in the place I'd begun to think of as mine—the bathroom. As the heat in my body flowed out, I unloaded my frustrations on him. The space between who I thought I really was and who the women at work imagined me to be grew.

I enjoyed being that normal person working hard for a paycheck, with the protective buffer of other women to make the workday bearable and, sometimes, especially when we pulled something over on Chester, fun. But the more they entrusted me with their stories and secrets, unexciting as they were, the more deceitful I felt.

I think Evan believed he was alleviating my concerns by simply and pragmatically talking me through what could be a usable newspaper story. As I spoke, I felt him editing my worries, the details of my newfound relationships, until only the simple facts remained. When we stopped talking, I felt nothing but the icy water tightening my skin, as if keeping me from guilt and obligation and confusion. The cold temperature made the heat outside the tub seem far away.

In bed at night, even with Evan beside me, I didn't fall asleep easily. I kept making up bizarre clues for *Pot o' Gold*'s puzzles, designing short answers with one-letter differences: home and hole, web and wed, rob and job. Other times I woke with letters, unattached to words or sentences, floating around me. Sometimes the letters came down like snow and fell into improper positions on the pages of puzzles.

And just as I was beginning to believe that, among the people I worked with or sent tiebreakers to, Martha was the only one who wasn't in some way damaged, either by poverty or a missing spouse or some type of physical aberration, I found out differently. Martha's mother called in sick for her on a Monday. The following day at lunch Joan told me the story. Talking softly to avoid being overheard by Chester, Joan revealed the details, some covered over by crinkling bags and scraping chairs. A year and a half earlier, Martha had had a nervous breakdown. Ever since her recovery, she'd suffered periodic anxiety attacks.

"You know how she spends a long time in the bathroom?" Joan asked. "Well, she's in there playing these tape recordings the psychiatrist gave her to calm her down."

"Why doesn't she just wear a Walkman?"

"She'd never take it off," said Joan. "She'd be all the time listening to her doctor comfort her instead of to us. And Chester . . ."

I took a deep breath and looked at the vulnerable women. "Probably the excitement of the wedding got to her," I said hopefully.

"Sure, that can set anyone off," said Sally Ann. "But it shouldn't make you stick a kitchen knife in your leg."

That night Evan got on my nerves. He didn't ask me how I was or how I felt when I got home from work. After I was in the tub, he handed me a Budweiser as usual and began pumping: Had I read any interesting letters? How much cash had we taken in? Did more entries come from the West Coast or from the southern states, specifically Florida?

The cold water relaxed me, and I began to confide in him. "What's weird is that no one who works at *Pot o' Gold* questions whether the puzzles are legitimate, and none of the contestants does either," I said.

"That's the tragedy," he said. "The human interest angle of this whole deal." He kissed me because he could tell I was sad. Then he got me another beer.

When the beer cap hit the floor, it sat grossly out of place in the design of the many small tiles. I realized what Evan had been doing all summer. He had been plying me with cold water and beer and sympathy. I was not upset to discover this. I was too hooked on the bathroom as my place of refuge.

"It would be using them," I said. "They'd lose their jobs if the story came out."

"But think of *all* those poor people being defrauded of hard-earned money because of this scam."

I didn't want to think; I just wanted to drink my beer. "It's not totally a scam," I said, refusing to admit that my job was not only worthless but wrong.

"Come on, Dara."

As he spoke my name, pulling it to him the way he did my body, I realized that I envisioned Evan as an escape from the suffocating world of responsibility, while he wanted me to be his partner in that workaday arena, which he never allowed himself to leave completely. And while my attitude wasn't likely to weather the demands of a lifetime commitment, it could be all-consuming. When I was touching him, I thought of nothing else.

Chester finally came through with the motive he'd had for hiring me. After work one evening he explained that he'd been moving me among different jobs so that I would know precisely what was required of each of the employees. He said he wanted me to be office manager. "Second in command," he announced with pride. When I hesitated, I saw that he was hurt. He said he'd had me in mind for the position from the start, due to the lines in my résumé that mentioned college, that he'd watched me for weeks and debated with himself my capability. When he said, "I like the way you handle yourself around the others," I knew he was on to me. He'd heard what I held back, what I told.

Evan saw my promotion as the key to a prize-winning story that would practically write itself. "Just breathe into the typewriter," he said dramatically, then danced around the room until the downstairs neighbor yelled through the hardwood floor.

"You tell me. I'll write. I have the notes already started," he said, circling me.

"I didn't say yes, Evan. I told him I'd think about it."

"You did good. String him along. Play it cool. Then, when he's got his head in the clouds, reel him in for the kill." Evan was excited; his metaphors were getting out of control.

"No, Evan," I cried. "No. No. No."

Evan stopped dancing.

He said, "You're right. OK." Then he stared at me and said, "Jesus. Of course. How could I be so stupid? You write the story, Dara. I'll help you for sure, but you write it. This could be your break. AP could even pick up the story if it's good enough."

I pictured my name in the *Times-Dispatch*, while Evan explained that we might have to share the byline. He wasn't sure he could get the paper to print a story by someone they didn't know. But he promised he'd check with the city editor immediately.

That night I dreamed of the possibilities. Stay, sway. Tell, sell. Storm, story. Lie, die.

Chester began to give me paychecks to stamp. While setting dollar amounts, I discovered that Joan and Martha and Sally Ann, who'd all worked at *Pot o' Gold* much longer than I had, didn't even make minimum wage. Joan had worked at the magazine for four years. The deaf sisters, no matter that they did the job of six people, received one check between them. But Chester had promised me a substantial raise as office manager.

I knew I couldn't tell Evan this. He'd no longer need hard proof that the *Pot o' Gold* games were phony to crack the story. He'd tell me I'd merely have to make a call to the labor board.

That evening after work was as hot as any all summer. People walked in slow motion to their cars, and from their cars into their houses. The sun, still high in the sky, bounced its heavy light off the buildings I passed on my way home.

As usual, Evan was beside the cold tub with beers. Even before I undressed, I told him I was quitting *Pot o' Gold*. I anticipated him objecting, yelling as he had the day I almost didn't take the job, telling me what an opportunity I was letting go by. Instead, he surprised me. He didn't say a thing. Though I'd given him no real encouragement, maybe he was thinking I'd still write the story. Or maybe he was right then beginning to formulate his own version in the same, silent way he functioned when he was working on something important. Of course, it may have just been too hot for him to get all worked up, because for the first time all summer, he climbed into the tub with me and slid his legs under mine. We fit.

Evan and I lay together there for a long time without talking or moving. The colors filtering through the skylight darkened and became part of the cold immersion. I felt caught and pressed down on all sides by the water. But I had no desire to get out. I put my head back against the tub's rim and waited for the bath to become as warm as the air around us.

Dancing with the Movies

Three people from California came ahead to check out the locals. The Californians sniffed at them, trailed them, and then, like animals marking unfamiliar territory, claimed Nelson Potter. Although he had a job with his father laying driveways, Nelson answered the ad in the *Nelsonville Pilot* for a location scout. He knew he could find the perfect spot where a sixteen-year-old might lose his virginity in the southern Maryland landscape, where a man and woman could meet secretly after dark, where on the water an accident would most likely occur if, say, someone was alone and unfamiliar with the ways of the Chesapeake Bay. The Californians' questions were easy ones, and Nelson answered with a confidence he'd never felt in four years at Nelsonville Senior High or in the nearly ten years since. His location suggestions were places where he felt at home—deep in old man Roberts's tobacco field, in the parking lot behind the Bus Stop Tavern on Main Street, at the uncertain tip of Maryland—that dangerous point of collision between Potomac and Chesapeake.

Micky Silver, a thirtyish thin man who wore sea green–rimmed glasses and short-sleeved, striped shirts, was head of production. He liked Nelson's location suggestions and wanted to know if he'd stay on during the shooting of the movie,

Hinterland. They were driving in Micky's rented white Lincoln to Calvert, the largest town in the area.

"This sure is an interesting part of the country," Micky said. Nelson wanted to tell Micky that he sure had an interesting job but was afraid he'd sound too small town, so he didn't say anything.

Nelson tried to imagine how Main Street appeared to an outsider and wondered if its worn storefronts and cracked walkways looked depressing or quaint. It was hard to tell with people, particularly with this group from Hollywood. Each shop hugged the next one in line, not giving up its tattered hold on earlier times. The street was so familiar to Nelson that he couldn't get a true picture of it. It was too comfortable, like wearing old, favorite clothes.

Once past Main Street, Nelson followed the thick dark roads, and watched down the thinner offshoots, some that his father had paved or rolled; always he looked out for something he knew about Nelsonville or something he could imagine.

"Here's the road to the crematorium," Nelson pointed out in case Micky needed that kind of information. Usually Micky said, "We *could* use that," to just about anything Nelson mentioned, but today Micky laughed.

"Just show me the way to Friendly Ford," he said as they neared the outskirts of town.

Field after tan field of corn and alfalfa fell off behind them. The highway stopped ducking around trees and straightened out, a direct line toward Calvert. They passed Stanner's, the department store where Nelson's mother had taken him every August for clothes to start off the school year, and the barbershop that once kept a pair of monkeys in its window to distract children from the clicking scissors.

Micky pulled into Friendly Ford. "What the hell's that?" he asked, referring to the building across the street. Nelson explained that the A&P had been turned into a bingo hall two years earlier. Advertisements for specially priced chicken and produce had been replaced by giant bingo cards covering the building's glass front. Nelson's mother played bingo every Thursday, and whenever she won, which was about once a month, she made a point of telling Nelson and his father that now she'd be contributing extra to her Christmas club. It could be May, but she'd advise her men to think about what they wanted for Christmas.

Micky didn't say anything when Nelson announced that his mom had won over a hundred dollars since January; he seemed anxious to get into the showroom of Friendly Ford.

"What do you think of this baby?" Micky asked Nelson. Micky moved his glasses onto his head, rubbed the bridge of his nose, and gestured toward a dark blue passenger van with two sky blue stripes across its sliding door. Nelson ran his hands over the pale upholstery and around the grooved steering wheel, then got in and slammed the door shut on the soft voices and ringing phone in the showroom. While Micky sat at a desk with the sales manager, Nelson stayed in the driver's seat of the van. Imagining traffic and then the quiet roads down by the bay, he touched the accessories one by one: the radio and tachometer, the cigarette lighter, the mirror on the underside of the passenger's visor.

"We're set, Nelson my man," said Micky. He placed his open palms on the vehicle's roof.

"You mean you bought it?" Nelson asked Micky as they walked out to the parking lot.

"I bought it," Micky said and lowered his face away from the sun.

"You could have rented it," Nelson suggested. His father had never bought a new car; he'd always bargained with Brucie Mott, who strolled the used car lot under a blizzard of colorful plastic flags.

"Listen, Nelson, I don't question how the studio wants to spend its money. I just follow policy."

Nelson drove the van carefully, checking in his rearview for Micky, who was following him back to Nelsonville. The new smell of the van and the new job made him light-headed and happy. Micky had explained that Nelson would be driving the crew and director to different locations; sometimes he'd be asked to run for materials and to pick up the movie stars at Dulles Airport. It beat the hell out of spreading gravel and pouring asphalt for driveways. In addition, Nelson was making lots more money than his father paid him.

"We have an important job, Son," Nelson's dad was careful to remind him, more often since Nelson had been working for the movie people. "Without us, families would never be sure they could get to their houses."

Once when Nelson was raking the three-quarter-inch stone for a ranch in Calvert, he'd considered what would happen if he went berserk and started stretching the stuff over lawns to connect each driveway to the next. From above, his creation would resemble one of those mazes in a kid's magazine, where the object is to find your way to the outside through a network of curves and dead ends. He pictured his father gently rubbing at the spot above his lip as he considered Nelson's deed, then breaking out with a stream of curses.

Nelson parked in the lot of the Ramada where Micky would be staying for the eight-week shoot. Built five years earlier in anticipation of a NASA plant that had since lost its funding, the Ramada normally didn't get much use, even though it was the most luxurious hotel around. Some of the rooms, it was claimed, had never been slept in.

"Come on in and have a beer with me," Micky said. Micky explained that he wasn't used to spending much time by himself. The two men who had arrived with him from California on this preliminary mission had flown in their wives the day before.

"Bring the map with you," Micky said. The map was Nelson's ticket to accompany Micky anywhere. It had originally gotten him the location scout job. Nelson had drawn the handmade, colored, finely detailed map of the town of Nelsonville and its surrounding areas himself, because none of the map-producing companies had come out with one, and there was no assurance they ever would. On Nelson's map, every shop and house in Nelsonville was accounted for.

Micky smiled at Sarah Jane behind the front desk as he walked into the lounge.

"Have one for me," she called.

Sarah Jane was blonde and leggy and had been a couple of grades behind Nelson in high school. Whenever he'd considered asking her out, he'd quickly dropped the idea because he worried over what they'd talk about. Finally they had an obvious connection—the movie. Nelson thought of driving with Sarah Jane in the brand-new van that, for a time, he could pretend was his own, as Micky, using the eraser end of his pencil, pointed out a purple X, like a small bruise, on Malory Lane. "What's this again?" he asked.

"That's where you said the guy buys the flowers in the scene where—" Nelson started.

"Right, right," Micky said. "How could I forget?"

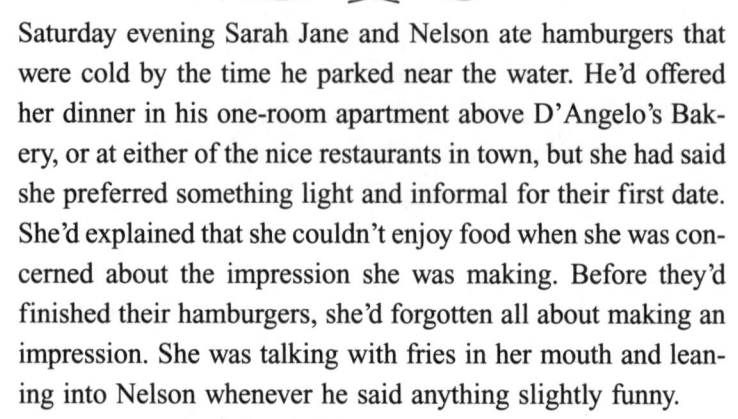

―――※―――

Saturday evening Sarah Jane and Nelson ate hamburgers that were cold by the time he parked near the water. He'd offered her dinner in his one-room apartment above D'Angelo's Bakery, or at either of the nice restaurants in town, but she had said she preferred something light and informal for their first date. She'd explained that she couldn't enjoy food when she was concerned about the impression she was making. Before they'd finished their hamburgers, she'd forgotten all about making an impression. She was talking with fries in her mouth and leaning into Nelson whenever he said anything slightly funny.

It was June but already close to 90 degrees. The two sat on rocks and talked while, a few feet away, bay water tapped gently at the shore. Sarah Jane asked if Nelson had brought any beer. When he shook his head, she asked if he wanted to go in for a dip. Nelson saw that Sarah Jane was someone who constantly tested limits; if he didn't say yes to one of her questions, she'd just press him with another.

Sarah Jane undid her pale pink cotton blouse, which buttoned up the back. He would have offered to help her but that would have overstepped the boundaries. All of Nelsonville's adolescents dipped into the Chesapeake on dark, warm, weekend nights. Usually the kids jumped in and swam in a group, but none of them ever grabbed or touched anyone else in play or in passion. The absence of outer clothes seemed to convey an aura of privacy. Afterward they'd go over to Heidi's Diner, where they'd order greasy hamburgers and chocolate Cokes. The marks of wet underwear would show through their clothing like a badge for a private club. But the most daring of the swimmers were the one or two, usually boys, who had no mark to prove they'd been swimming—because they'd slipped under the water without wearing any clothes at all. Nelson guessed that Micky would have been one of the unmarked boys if he'd grown up in Nelsonville.

Sarah Jane unzipped her jeans casually and smoothly pulled them from her legs, then looked out toward the dark Chesapeake as if she stood alone in a dressing room with a silky dress that would soon glide over her body. Her underwear was flesh colored, and when Nelson finally looked directly at her, he thought for a minute that she might be as fearlessly naked as one of those boys whose clothes showed no water stains.

Hopping on one leg, then the other, Nelson peeled *his* pants off. Still staring off at the water, Sarah Jane asked if it would be hard going back to the old job with his father after working for the movies, and Nelson said he didn't know.

"Say the word 'movies' and you've got yourself a ticket to just about anywhere in town," he said. She nodded agreement. Her hair was very fine and skimmed the line of her jaw. Nelson explained how his dad had been skeptical.

"Could be one of them porno movies," he'd said. But once Nelson got the job and found out that the movie starred David Taylor, everyone was all for Nelson's new temporary occupation.

"I know what you mean," she said. "People I haven't talked to in years are asking me if I've actually spoken to him on the phone and what room he's going to be staying in."

Nelson stood in white briefs—the only light around—with his hands at his sides, and then followed Sarah Jane into the water. "Be careful here," he told her, and held himself from taking her hand. "This is where the currents cross." In the darkness he didn't want her moving too far off. The bay and the Potomac smacked together, and when the clouds passed, a fine reflection of moonlight caught the silvery spray.

Witnessing that collision briefly spotlighted by the moon, Nelson hoped that in some way he'd be changed by the movie coming to his town. Hollywood had chosen Nelsonville to be the backdrop to a story of romance and intrigue. He had never imagined that the town where he'd always lived would turn into a big deal.

The cool water whooshed around their bodies as they walked deeper into the liquid darkness. Nelson heard Sarah Jane dip all the way in and swim off. Noiselessly, he lowered his body, then his head, under water. When he came up, Sarah Jane stood beside him. Then she surprised him by hanging her arms loosely around his neck. She said, "I just love being with someone in the movie business," stretching the word "love" into two syllables. The gesture was so sexless that Nelson didn't even try to kiss her.

Back on shore they took turns dabbing at their faces and legs with a blanket. When they were in their clothes again and heading for the car, she said, "Nelson. Were you named after Nelsonville?"

Nelson told her, as he did everyone who tried to make the connection, that he was named for his great-grandfather from West Virginia. "Nelsonville, that's just a coincidence," he said, though he'd never been totally convinced that his mother hadn't given him the name simply to keep him from leaving home.

On the ride back to Sarah Jane's house, she talked about the movie stars who would be arriving in Nelsonville in a week or two. They wondered how tall David Taylor really was, if Mary

Birch was a vegetarian, if Frank Reynolds and Jessica Flynn were still having the affair that Sarah Jane had read about in a magazine left behind in a Ramada room.

"See ya, Nelson," she called, as if they'd been going out together for years, and skipped off down the black driveway of her parents' house. He waited until she got to the front door before he took the van out of neutral. In the porch light, the signs of the swim were visible; the wet patches from her underwear and dripping hair made a see-through pattern on her blouse.

He didn't pull away from the house until the front porch light went out and the hallway lamp went on, then that light, too, was replaced by the small gold square of an upstairs window, which must have been her bedroom. Nelson could have watched a movie made of Sarah Jane, just the house light following her blonde hair.

"Well, look who's Mr. Good Mood this morning," Nelson's mother said, pouring him a glass of orange juice. Although he wasn't working with his father these days, he continued to observe the habit of eating breakfast with his parents as if he were about to go off to lay driveways.

His mother's hair, tightly curled, was shiny and still smelled of the beauty parlor. She wore a shade of lipstick she told Nelson was called Sunset. His father eyed her as she delivered plates of scrambled eggs and bacon to the table.

"What's the occasion?" Nelson's father asked. He buttered his toast, then stroked it with thick swipes of grape jelly.

"I'm going to get an autograph today," she said, winking at Nelson.

She wanted David Taylor's autograph. Nelson was picking

him up in an hour and a half at the airport. The actor would be joining the crew and some of the other stars who had arrived earlier in the week. Nelson's mother wanted to get to him before he grew tired of giving autographs.

"Annie can't keep up with all the hairdos the ladies want this week," she said, proud that she'd been able to secure an appointment.

"I'll see you on my lunch hour," she said, wiping the kitchen counter and finding her purse. "Ramada Inn," she specified. "Will I be able to find parking?"

Nelson's mother sorted the mail and operated the switchboard for a large press, which printed items like canned food labels and advertisements on matchbooks. His two older brothers had moved out of town as soon as they'd graduated from high school—Georgie married a girl five years older and bought a trailer in Florida; Carl went to Alaska. Whenever Nelson would come on his mother crying softly to herself with some magazine propped deceptively in front of her face, he was sure she was missing the brothers, who seldom called or visited.

"I'll get the autograph," Nelson offered.

"We've been over this," she said, smiling. For some reason the autograph would have more value if she obtained it herself. "Besides, I want to take a look at that Sarah Jane you've been seeing so much of."

She winked at Nelson again and started for the front door.

"What's that?" Nelson's father asked.

"I told you," she called from the porch steps. The screen door slammed behind her.

"I must have been asleep when you told me," Nelson's dad called back to her above the commotion. Then he turned and looked at Nelson for an answer.

"I've been seeing Sarah Jane Barrett," Nelson said between bites of toast.

His father put his fingers on his chin and tilted his head back. Finding what he'd been looking for in his memory, he said, "I put her folks' driveway in before you were born."

"Well, I'm off," Nelson said.

"They let you go like that?" he asked, pointing at Nelson's jeans.

"Sure," Nelson said. "You think this is bad. You should see the way some of the actors dress."

Nelson's father shook his head at Nelson's appearance, explaining that his son should wear a uniform or, at the least, a suit, when transporting Hollywood's stars.

"You don't look any better than when you work for me," he said and vigorously stirred his coffee.

Although he had overheard his father bragging to Uncle Pete in Baltimore about the movie crew job, Nelson knew his dad would be relieved when they were laying driveway together again and Nelson was done with "funny ideas about running off to Hollywood."

Shrugging his shoulders, Nelson went out to the van, which he'd washed the afternoon before. All week he'd been making trips to Dulles Airport to pick up actors and other people associated with the movie. Some of them wore caps, stiff colorful ones, not genuine dusty seed caps; some of the men were shorter than he'd imagined they'd be; some of the women were louder. With their jewelry and their expensive suitcases and the way their voices lifted in question even if they weren't asking a question, they seemed to have arrived from a foreign country. A country where no one worried about money because there was plenty to go around.

A sign labeled "Hinterland," which Nelson held up at the appropriate gate, had attracted the tech people and the writers like bait. Because the actors, even the lesser-known ones, wanted to be recognized immediately, Nelson had tried to study their promo shots to be sure he'd know who was who. But today he was picking up David Taylor, and there would be no mistaking him.

People were on their way to work or preparing to open their shops as Nelson drove through town. Banners, which normally came out twice a year, once for the firemen's carnival in July and once for a crab feast at the end of the summer, now stretched a new message between the streetlights: WELCOME TO NELSONVILLE, HOLLYWOOD. There had been a big discussion over the comma, with Mrs. Gress, Nelson's junior high English teacher, being its principal proponent.

Everything pointed toward something big happening in town. The Woolworth's window shone, it was so clean. Todd's Texaco displayed "Howdy Hollywood" signs next to the pumps, and the price of gas had been raised two cents a gallon. Al Golden had started the welcoming campaign the week before when he'd set a sign outside his diner saying "Movie-Maker Special—Corned Beef Today." Nelson wasn't sure if everyone could get the special or if you had to be from Hollywood. And what about someone who swung between the two? Could Nelson order the Filmmakers' Two Fried Eggs for $1.19 that Al usually charged $1.59 for? Nelson's mother said that Al had the right idea, but Nelson knew about the catering truck that was Al's competition. Hired by the film company, the truck hummed constantly behind the Ramada and followed the actors and crew to each location to deliver plates of cold cuts, breads, and sliced fresh fruit. The truck was the size of the one that delivered to the Super Giant supermarket in Calvert.

Already carpenters hired by the film company were at work on the Bus Stop Tavern. They were building a raised patio where people could drink outside, the necessary building permits displayed prominently on the tavern door. Rumor was that when filming began in the bar, Dan Fraker, the owner, would get $1,000 a night as well as the new addition. There was initially some commotion over money when Bob Corhey was offered $1,200 for just four hours' use of his store. The difference, Bob argued, was due to the inconvenience of having his front window, with "General Store" painted on the glass, shot out during one of the movie's violent scenes.

David Taylor had already deplaned by the time Nelson showed up at the gate. Surrounded by a group of mostly female fans, he was easy to pick out.

"Sorry," Nelson said, quickly directing him out of the crowd and toward the airport parking lot.

David Taylor was thinner than Nelson had imagined, a good ten years older than he, and ruggedly handsome. Although David wore jeans, a T-shirt, and a cotton cardigan with the sleeves pushed toward his elbows, Nelson sensed that this casual attire was different from his own, and more expensive for sure. Trying to illustrate a point for Nelson earlier in the week, Micky had mentioned that *his* shirt had cost sixty dollars.

When Nelson slid the side van door open, the actor threw his bags in and grabbed the front door handle. Once inside the van, David asked, "How's it going?" speaking to Nelson for the first time.

"Pretty good. I ran into quite a bit of traffic when I got close to D.C."

Soon Nelson was driving along roads flanked on either side by fields of new corn. Later, there would be tobacco.

"I can't remember the last time I was in the South," David said.

"I can't either," Nelson said, trying to be funny. Most people Nelson knew didn't consider Maryland the real South.

David asked what people in Nelsonville did for fun.

"Bus Stop Tavern," Nelson said, and went on to describe the addition. "The Stop," he clarified. He also mentioned the pool hall and bowling alley in Calvert and, of course, the Chesapeake Bay. While he didn't sneer, David somehow didn't seem interested. Nelson tried to imagine what David did when he wasn't acting. Probably Nelsonville was pretty boring with none of the clubs and glitzy restaurants of California.

When Nelson found a rock station on the radio, the actor put his head back against the seat and smiled. Nelson was unsure whether to ask him about music or keep his mouth shut and drive.

The road hummed along underneath them, and even though it was just after noon, David fell asleep against the door of the van. For a minute, Nelson imagined that he could drive anywhere. He could deliver the actor to his mother at the Calvert Press, or to Al Golden's diner in time for the luncheon special, or to Annie's Beauty Parlor, where a dozen women would coo from under the huge, growling hair dryers. "Nelson, what a surprise," they'd say.

"Here we are," Nelson said, tentatively touching David on the shoulder.

"The Ramada," David said as if he were answering a question, while Nelson jumped out and came around to retrieve the two leather bags. As David followed him into the lobby and across the soft red carpet, Nelson felt important. He showed the star to the reception desk and nodded at Sarah Jane stationed there.

Nelson spotted his mother gripping her pencil and an unmistakable piece of Calvert Press stationary. Her face was flushed the way it got just before the relatives came to visit. "Uh," Nelson said, nudging David lightly, "there's a lady who looks real anxious to have your autograph."

Everyone wanted to be an extra, Sarah Jane was saying over a beer at the Stop. The people from Nelsonville said "extra" like the end of the word had leaves: ex-tree.

"Suzie's going to be taking the money for shoes in the bowling scene over at Big Bowl. And her mom's the cashier at the concession stand," said Sarah Jane. She named half a dozen more people she'd gone to school with who were appearing in nonspeaking parts during the shooting of *Hinterland*. Everybody in town seemed to have a new job. It was as if someone had come through Nelsonville and said there had been a mix-up, that everybody was in the wrong job. Overnight, Nelsonville's plumbers had become bartenders, beauticians had turned into waitresses, shop owners had become members of a jury, and gravel men had been transformed into chauffeurs. Somehow, playing a cashier in the movies made a person feel like a bank president.

Sometimes Nelson waited around while David watched the dailies. As the actor grimaced or smiled over the replay of the day's shooting, Nelson reminded himself where he'd been standing or sitting during a particular scene: as Mrs. Gress, playing a clerk at Todd's Texaco, handed David his change from a fill-up, Nelson had leaned against the van just out of range of the movie camera. When David was filmed running into the Chesapeake, with Mary Birch charging after him, Nelson had his shoes off and was wading along the shore, comfortably out of bounds.

Those townspeople who weren't a part of the set tried to arrange the next best thing—to be near the stars in town. At the supermarket or Rexall Drugs or a red light. Sarah Jane was explaining how people called the Ramada all day for clues to the stars' whereabouts. "Any chance David Taylor will be heading for the post office?" Last week Nelson's own mother, without giving her name, had called Sarah Jane to see if Mary Birch was in her room. Mary wore lots of bracelets, which moved up and down both her arms when she tried to make a point.

"Mrs. Parma is dying to run into Frank Reynolds," Sarah Jane said, her lips a dark pink. Nelson reached for her hand. Mrs. Parma was a widow who gave lessons in "How to Strip for Your Husband," each Saturday in her club basement.

"She told me to swear to call when he was back in his room," she went on. "Like I've got nothing better to do." Although she pretended to be bothered by the inquiries, Nelson was certain that Sarah Jane enjoyed working for the Ramada these days. She'd told him the room-service bills the stars ran up were stupendous.

"Sarah Jane," he said, looking at her across a table at the Stop. His voice was cut off by the loud fan sitting on the windowsill. "Sarah Jane," he said again. "I wonder what you'd think of me taking a couple of courses at the community college." The longer Nelson stayed away from handling gravel, the more he thought of doing other things.

"Sarah Jane?" he said, but she was looking up at the door. Nelson focused in the direction of her stare and saw David Taylor and Laura Blartner, one of Sarah Jane's girlfriends. All the while Laura led the actor to a table near the back of the room, she smiled at her friends in the bar as if she were on a beauty pageant runway. With her hair all fixed up and her nails painted bright red, Laura appeared a lot more excited than David.

"Well," Nelson said, not knowing what else to say.

"I'll be right back," said Sarah Jane, making a beeline for Laura's table, where the couple nodded and smiled. David looked a little sleepy.

Nelson ordered another beer before Sarah Jane returned holding an eight-by-ten glossy of David like it was her ticket to success. "I could never ask him while I was on the desk," she said, referring to the Ramada's reception area. "It seemed like too unprofessional or something," she said, studying the inscription, "To Sarah Jane, of Nelsonville."

"Tomorrow night he'll be in here with somebody else," Nelson said. "That's how these guys operate." Nelson had seen David on the set when he'd handed Patty Moore and Patty's mother photos. He had squeezed each of their hands and stared at them good and long. Instead of disillusioning her, Nelson's words seemed to encourage Sarah Jane, as if she imagined bringing David to this very table in a night or two.

"Come on," Nelson said, draining his beer. He couldn't believe somebody bringing headshots into the Spot. "Let's get out of here."

Without arguing, Sarah Jane followed him to the van. They didn't say anything, and Nelson pulled a warm Bud out of the six-pack behind the seat and just drove. He followed the roads that on his map looked like colored lines, but now felt alive and familiar. The night was very dark, yet he drove fast, sensing he wouldn't be hurt because, after all, Hollywood was here.

The tree leaves bent back and moved with the wind the van made in passing. That was how it worked; the place where you lived made way for you, and you, in turn, made way for it. Lately though, with the movies, the town seemed to have forgotten this arrangement.

"You ever think of getting out?"

"While you're driving this fast? You've got to be kidding," Sarah Jane answered.

"Getting out of Nelsonville. Do you ever think about it?"

Sarah Jane sighed and said that she used to think about moving to somewhere like Texas. "And lately I've been thinking about it again," she said. "Florida, maybe. My uncle says he's heard they're planning to make a lot of movies in Florida."

Nelson spoke without adjusting his thoughts to accommodate Sarah Jane. "The movies come in, shift the town all around. People you normally see only on TV are suddenly pissing next to you in the bathroom. The focus of things changes. And you start to think everything can come this close."

"Nelson, are you drunk or what?"

Nelson pulled off the side of the road and cut the lights.

"What's wrong?" Sarah Jane asked. Nelson set the parking brake, got out and opened the side of the van, and, after collapsing one of the seats, spread an old Army blanket of his dad's across the floor. He led Sarah Jane back before she could ask if he had this or that or if he wanted to do something else. She didn't say anything. As they made love for the first time, Nelson called out her name and whispered everything he'd give her, but she didn't really seem to be with him no matter how hard or soft he held her and tried to get her around him.

Afterward, he heard a strange sound that, after a few minutes, he recognized as rain. It hadn't rained all month, and the grass was dry and brittle, the small corn shrinking into itself. The droplets pinged off the roof like something far off had broken apart.

"Sarah Jane?" Nelson's voice sounded hollow and not totally his own.

"Mmmmm?"

"What would you think if I was to try out to be an ex-tree?"

Nelson didn't see Sarah Jane much between the night in the van and the week he started carting all the Hollywood people back to the airport. His mother said she thought Sarah Jane had gone out with Micky Silver; one of Annie's hairdressers had spotted them at the miniature golf course outside of Calvert.

Sometimes Sarah Jane would call from the Ramada to say one of the actors was checking out and needed transportation to Dulles. They never exchanged small talk or gossip, only the facts of flight times to California.

The morning Nelson was to drive Micky to the airport, his mother handed him a freshly ironed short-sleeved shirt and slacks. A paisley tie was draped over the shirt hanger.

"I thought you'd want to look decent your last day," she said proudly. "You can go change in your old room."

"For Christ's sake, I'm not going to a funeral," Nelson said. Then he felt bad for snapping at her so he wore the clothes, but took off the tie as soon as he got to the Ramada.

"Nelson, my man," Micky said on the drive to the airport, "the producers have the final say and I hope they go for it, but don't count on it. A dance scene breaks the tone of the ending." Micky was talking about the footage of the wrap party, which celebrated the completion of the shooting of *Hinterland*. All of the residents of Nelsonville, along with the actors and tech people, had attended the dance. Micky and the director had discussions about the ending of the movie, and the director had grimaced when Micky suggested that the dance sequence could be tacked on as a thank you for the use of

Nelsonville. "That's what we have credits for," the director had said.

⌒⌒⌒

Before Micky boarded the plane he handed Nelson a wad of folded bills. "Good luck, Nelson," he said. "This sure is an interesting part of the country."

Generally, they didn't leave much behind. The Stop now had its raised patio and an awning that had been added because Mary Birch hadn't wanted to be photographed in "brash, direct sunlight." Al Golden had framed and hung headshots of all the actors, whether they'd wandered into his diner or not. Annie named her most popular haircut the Hinterlander.

After things got back to normal—Nelson on driveways, Sarah Jane checking in newlyweds, CRAB FEAST '90 replacing the Hollywood welcome banner—Nelson asked Sarah Jane if she wanted to go over to Ocean City for the weekend. She said she'd think about it.

And that was the way with everyone in town. Nobody had much energy to make decisions. Weighed down with anticipation, they all seemed to be waiting around for the movie to come out. Nelson was especially anxious to see if they were all in it at the very end, if the names of the cameramen and editors and the town itself might roll up and over their legs and bodies and faces.

But *Hinterland* never made it to Nelsonville. There were reports that it had played briefly in places like New York and Chicago, but no one knew anyone who'd seen it until it came out on video a year and a half after it had been shot.

Dan Fraker rented the movie first and showed it at the Stop one Saturday. Laura Blartner sat with her old boyfriend; Mrs. Gress shared a table up front with Mrs. Parma; Nelson's parents talked with Al Golden; Nelson stood in the back. Even though the place was packed as *Hinterland* began, all Nelson could hear were mugs of beer bumping the tabletops.

For the first time, Nelson saw the film in its proper order, and for the first time the sequence of specific events made sense. Nelson forgot where he had been and what he'd been doing during the scenes, and followed the images of the stars through the story.

Micky was right, Nelson thought, a dance finale with all the people of Nelsonville wouldn't have made much sense—and yet, it would have been great. Everybody who rented the movie, maybe even his brothers in Florida and Alaska, would have seen Nelsonville celebrating with the Hollywood stars. Nelson's mom in a new lavender dress and his dad with a paisley tie like Nelson's, David Taylor and Mary Birch with her bracelets, Frank Reynolds and Jessica Flynn, Mrs. Gress and Al Golden, all of them, dancing.

Even Nelson would have been included, not standing just out of camera range rubbing fingerprints from the van, but dancing with Sarah Jane as the cameras focused and clicked along with their movements, as the dangling microphones picked up every sound and the brightest lights pointed them out. Nelson imagined their spot as if it were marked with an X on his handmade map. In the slow fadeout, with Sarah Jane in his arms and the music moving him and all of Nelsonville, Nelson had found the place he wanted to live in forever.

Panama

Sometime after midnight, Ed Veal, our neighbor from down the street, brings him in. On the way up to his room, the hard plastic tips on the suitcase I gave him smack the steps. Mom and Pop must be throwing on every light upstairs because a strip of brightness even slips under my door. I hear Pop slap him on the back and Mom say she's going to put on some eggs. He says he just wants to go to bed.

None of us expected him until morning, but that's the way these things go. I pretend I don't hear any of this. When he raises his voice to explain the plane trip home, the reason he's early, and why he called Ed instead of disturbing them in the middle of the night, Mom says, "Shhh. Your sister." I picture all of them looking at my bedroom door.

Finally, Ed goes home and the lights are turned out and Tommy moves around in the creaky metal bed in the room right next to mine. Mom coughs a couple of times; Pop says something low and mumbling that I can't make out. Then it's quiet again.

I keep my eyes open in the darkness and wonder what Tommy will be like this time. When he came home right after basic training, he walked around in a trance. Like he didn't know any of us, like he didn't know his own name or anything. That was when we saw him. Most of the time he just slept.

I did get through to him one time though, and he told me about this kid who'd cracked up. The kid started jumping up and down on food in the mess hall. Told people to throw him anything they couldn't eat and he'd stomp on it. Tommy said he rolled an orange across the floor. The kid jumped on the orange until the MPs led him away.

The fact that it's afternoon and Tommy hasn't even stirred means that this visit may not be all that different from the other one. One thing's not the same anyway—it was fall when he came home after basic. Certain things had been decided: the Baltimore Orioles had blown their chances to be in the playoffs; I had Mrs. Seltzer for social studies; Tommy was going to Panama. This time nothing's firmed up. The trees are only beginning to thicken for summer. Sheets on the line in the backyard crack against air scented with forsythia, cut grass, a coming storm.

"We'll let him sleep a little longer," Mom says as she comes into the living room in her blue and white apron. She has her hair done in loose black curls this morning. She winks at me and says it might be nice if I put on the new dress I wore at Easter. Like she's got to tell me everything. The family's coming over at three for roast beef dinner, because Mom likes to celebrate with a feed bag. "It's the least I can do," she says, walking off and lightly patting the back of her hair.

Actually, I'd be just as happy to take a plate of food to my room and listen to WCAO. Talk to Tommy when he's alone. Except that this whole deal is for him, after all. His head's probably going to be all shaved again to look like some huge, weird pear.

Pop paces around the living room until he finally turns on the

Oriole game. Looking above him to where Tommy's room is, Pop says to me, "Why don't you call up there? See if he's awake."

Pop gets nervous like this when Tommy phones from Panama, too. I think because my father feels responsible. Tommy didn't even want to go into the service, but Pop kept hammering away about duty and glory and invaluable, marketable skills. Right. As a last resort, Pop relied on Uncle Billy to tell Tommy how it really was in the army.

"Go on, give a call up there," Pop insists.

I go to the bottom of the steps and holler, "Tommy, come on. Get up. I want to hear about Panama." After a groan, he says something indistinguishable. What if he gets like Kim Solby's brother who went to Vietnam? When Darren came home he didn't say much; he never had, so nobody worried at first. Then, for a while, he didn't finish his sentences. Finally, he stopped talking altogether and grew fat as an overstuffed armchair. "Too bad about that Solby boy," Pop used to say.

Panama. The strange thing about Panama is Tommy's not always there. My theory is that Panama's just the word they tell the guys to use with their families when they're really someplace else. Sort of like when I say I'm at Kim's.

Once when we hadn't heard from Tommy in about eight weeks, he called to say he'd been training in the jungle. Later he wrote in a letter to me that he'd been to Honduras. He can't say these things on the phone. When I press him, he says, "No comment." I bet he's been on secret missions to Nicaragua and El Salvador and maybe even Bolivia. I read the papers. I started reading page one of the *Evening Sun* right after Tommy made Airborne and got his infantry assignment to Panama. "About time," was all my father said when he caught me reading. He's a union printer at the paper.

Right after the inning's over, Pop stands up and says loudly, "Come on, son. Your mother has dinner going. We've got the family coming over." He looks at me and says, "Damn those Birds. Can't even get a hit."

"Uncle Billy?" Tommy calls.

"Yes, Uncle Billy's coming," says Pop loudly. Uncle Billy's driving up from Williamsburg. Uncle Billy served in Korea before Tommy and I were born, but he gave us chopsticks that he told us were authentic. Tommy and I sharpened them into swords.

About ten minutes later, I hear the shower going, the droplets bouncing wildly off everything. Off my brother's body.

A little later he comes slowly down the stairs. I try to sit still and not jump out of my skin. He looks bigger. His hair's actually long enough to tell it's dark brown. Wearing his uniform, he's the color of the spruces that kids hide behind when they're sneaking cigarettes in back of the high school. "Hey," Tommy says and smiles at me.

I just can't help myself. I run into his partly open arms and squeeze him. "Tommy," I say so softly that he probably doesn't hear me. His stomach and arms are hard. The stiff shirt scratches my face and the shiny buttons are cold as pieces of ice. He smells different, like boys at the school dances—a combination of soap and aftershave. Tommy doesn't ruffle my hair but taps my head carefully.

"So," he says when I finally stand back from him. "So," he says again after a minute, and rubs his hand across his chin and face in one swipe, the way Pop does.

"Your sister's got a job after school," Pop says, putting his hands in his pockets. "Tell him, Val."

"Yeah, I got this job at Joe's Dairy Bar. I can work there full-time after school's out next month." I describe how to make the best-tasting milkshakes, and about the time I slid a Gummy Rat into a hot dog bun and served it to Kim when she came in with her new boyfriend. Tommy doesn't laugh as hard as I thought he would.

"Next year's the last one?" he asks. Like he doesn't know how old I am. I nod yes, and Tommy asks Pop the baseball score.

"What did you do in Honduras?" I ask Tommy.

Without looking away from the game Tommy says, "Guarding." At the commercial, he elaborates. "All we were doing was guarding the communications there. You know, TV, radio stations. The stations are on this hill. All we did was walk around."

"With guns?" I ask.

"Sure, with guns," Pop answers. He turns up the volume on the game.

Mom's wiping her hands on her apron when she comes into the living room. She kisses Tommy on the cheek and tells him Ed's called three times already. "Come help me with the beef," she says to Pop. "They'll be here before long. You kids have your hands washed?"

I look at my brother's hands and wonder if he's ever used a rifle. I mean on somebody. Or if somebody's aimed at him. Kim's brother, before he stopped talking, described moving lizardlike across the ground, his gun always as close as another limb on his body. He said sometimes everything in sight seemed like the enemy. Even the poor slob right in front of you.

"Mona," Mom practically sings when she opens the front door to the company. Within ten minutes all the relatives are here. They coo and hug one another, then step back. Uncle Arthur says he's glad the weather cleared up. Mom nudges me. "I thought I told you to put on a dress." Uncle Billy shakes

Tommy's hand hard, then covers it with his other hand. With a Kleenex, Aunt Sarah dabs at the corners of her eyes.

Mom seats us around the table and the picture is complete: Grandmother at one end and Tommy at the other. On either side are Uncle Billy, Pop, Mom, and me, then Aunt Mona and Uncle Arthur, Aunt Sarah and Uncle Fred. After grace Mom asks Tommy what kind of food he eats in Panama. Tommy reports that when he's off base, seafood and chili dogs are best, that meat and pizza are for the birds.

"What kind of bugs do they have there?" I ask, taking a huge spoon of succotash.

"Fire ants, a lot of chiggers, mosquitoes the size of bullets," Tommy says, without looking up.

"Did you get sick from the water, honey?" Aunt Sarah asks. A Kleenex tucked in the long sleeve of her dress points at her fingers as she eats.

"No," he says. "I'm immune now. Got used to it."

"That's the boy," says Pop. He lifts the platter of meat and sends it on a second round.

"What about animals?" I want to find the right word or look to take Tommy back to the roadway of books we wound through the rooms of this house. Once they led under this very table, then covered with a sheet, where I pretended I was the nurse who brought him back to life after he'd crossed the desert. Another time, in an empty refrigerator box, he pressed my arm with a match-heated quarter that branded me for days.

We played our favorite game when nobody was home but the two of us. We pulled the two big cushions from the living room sofa. On the floor, between our separate territories, we left a space—an imaginary, treacherous, fast-moving river. Sometimes we each lined up the same number of small plastic men or animals at our respective edges, then blew at them or dropped Pop's bowling ball on the floor beside them to see how many would fall in and drown. The weird thing was, we didn't always remember whose side the plastic bodies had been on. And usually we fought about that.

Tommy finally looks up. "I've got some pictures. Go upstairs," he says to me. Then he adds, "No, I better go." While Tommy's away from the table, Mom brings out a blueberry pie and a lemon meringue pie and coffee.

Tommy passes photos around the table. There are sloths and armadillos and boys in T-shirts. Everything seems green or white. Then Tommy pulls things from a brown paper bag. The women get change purses, each the shape of a different animal's head with a mouth that snaps open and shut.

"That's a crocodile, Aunt Mona," Tommy says. Aunt Mona lets Uncle Arthur open it for her. The uncles dangle key chains with pineapples or coconuts attached. Tommy hands Mom a white plastic purse with a map of the Canal Zone detailed on the front, while I unfold a T-shirt with a colorful bird at its center.

"The lady told me it would shrink," says Tommy when I hold the large piece of black cloth against my chest for the others to see. I picture Tommy's big hands filing through racks of shirts to find one I'd like.

Pop examines the T-shirt Tommy's given him, then clears his throat. When it looks like he's not going to display the shirt, I push back my chair and bend to look. There's an outline of a Rambo-looking guy lifting a lady over his shoulder. You can't see the lady's face, only the backs of her long legs in seamed stockings and her behind like a heart. In the man's other hand is a rifle. Before I can read the name of the bar that this shirt advertises, Pop turns the shirt toward Uncle Billy, who winks at Pop. "You been here, son?" Pop asks Tommy.

"No comment," says Tommy with a grin.

"More coffee?" Mom asks around.

Uncle Fred, his glasses sliding down on his nose, says, "Well, Tommy tell us what's been the most exciting thing that's happened to you in Panama."

Tommy doesn't hesitate. He doesn't miss a beat. "The first time I got laid."

Forks scraping at pie plates, teaspoons clinking in coffee cups stop. Nobody moves. A noise like air being let out of a beach ball comes from somewhere. I can't believe it. I can't lift my eyes up from my plate to see if Tommy's proud or embarrassed.

Not that long ago, Tommy didn't like anybody to hear him burp. He wouldn't let Mom in the bedroom when he was changing his shirt. Whole nights, Tommy and I giggled over things we would never say out loud.

Finally, Uncle Billy clears his throat. Mom takes this as a cue to leave the table. Under her breath, Grandmother says, "My."

The women gather dishes and whisper. Sniffling and touching china to china, they move from the dining room to the kitchen. Without speaking, Mom demonstrates to Grandmother how to load the dishwasher, while Aunt Mona and Aunt Sarah scrape the food that's left into plastic containers that snap shut. Behind them, Uncle Billy slowly starts to close the door to the den. In his other hand is a bottle of Jim Beam that he lifts toward Tommy. From deep inside, the men laugh and laugh. When I close my eyes, I can hear gunfire.

Beds

*W*aiting for me at Penn Station in Baltimore, my father shifts his weight and runs coins, deep in his pocket, through his fingers. I know this because I've waited with him on the same platform for my brother, Peter.

As soon as I step off the train my father calls, "Hey, Annie baby. Over here. How was your trip?" He gives me a squeeze and takes my canvas bag, so worn that it has a fuzzy look. Stepping around the still, dark hollows of rain, I follow him through the parking lot as he wonders aloud where he parked the old Pontiac.

When the train left Boston the sky was full of snow. Lakes and fields and houses lost their color right in front of me. About Philadelphia the rain started, first a series of fine dots. Then the hundreds of points ran together on the train window to make the hard plastic look scratched by a very sharp knife. From then on, everything was as dark and wet as one huge puddle.

"Here we go," he says, pulling his car keys through the coins in his pocket. Unlocking the trunk, he looks back at my hands. "This all you got with you?"

After we are in the car Dad says, "I feel like a regular chauffeur today. Boy oh boy." He laughs and explains how earlier he picked up Peter and Lisa at the airport. "They're staying over tonight, too. Then tomorrow we'll all drive down to Richmond for the party."

Five days earlier, Peter had married Lisa Cantrell in Las Vegas. "It was some singles vacation package," my mother had explained on the phone. "He called me and said, 'Mom, I'm married. I met the most wonderful girl.' I said, 'This makes four times you met her.' He said, like he always does, 'This time is different.' Why does he keep doing this to himself? And to us—your father and me?" Then my mother started to cry. When I told her I'd come down for the wedding party Lisa's mother was giving, my mother stopped crying. I heard her strike a match, pictured her inhaling a Winston.

Peter's wives—news of them, anyway—are about the only change this part of Baltimore sees these days. Back when my brother and I were kids, some new house was always going up, some stranger moving in, another field was cleared and scraped and squared off into identical size lots. Finally, everything fit together like a giant jigsaw puzzle, and stayed that way.

As Dad drives with the radio on, I look at the soft whiteness coming from inside anonymous living rooms. I can't make out the colors of the raised ranch houses or the cold gray of the chain-link fence I know surrounds each one.

"How's school?" he asks, keeping his eyes on the dark road.

"Good," I say. "It's OK."

At night, when I was very young, sometimes I'd kneel on my bed and look into the forest behind my parents' house. Now that black space is covered with squares of house light. But back then, when there was only darkness, I imagined animal eyes staring back at me. I knew that animals lived and lurked between the lengths of oak and maple and evergreen. The creatures ate the carrots and bread I set at the edge of the woods, and they left signs behind—a pile of leaves, a hole in the earth. The wild animals, once close enough to steal our painted Easter eggs, were pushed farther back with each new row of houses that was built. And now the suburbs, huge and endless, have pressed those animals into memory. The funny thing is, except for an occasional turtle or a nest of abandoned baby bunnies, I don't remember seeing the animals, only knowing they were close by.

"Guess you'll be glad to be home for a few days," my father says. As Dad turns down the street that is the most familiar to me of all the streets like it, he says, "I almost forgot. Wait'll you hear this. I bought it with some money your Aunt Elaine gave me for my birthday." His hands look small as he pushes a couple of buttons under the dashboard. The first few notes of "Bad, Bad Leroy Brown" sound out down the street lined with quiet houses, silent cars. "It's a horn," he says.

I've heard these horns from classrooms and from the office I work in part-time, and wondered what could happen to a city if just half of the drivers had them. I never imagined my father with a multitrumpet musical air horn. I never figured him with anything but the TV.

My mother's at the door when he pulls up next to the house. The curb feeler scrapes a sound I've never forgotten.

"Jesus, Leroy," she says, giving me a hug, "you've got the dogs started." Dog barking echoes through the neighborhood. "Can you believe that horn? I feel like I've got a kid living home again instead of a . . . a . . . grown husband."

"An old husband, she meant to say," Dad says softly and winks at me. He heads for the bathroom.

The rooms in my parents' fourth-from-the-corner house never change. The rockers on a child's red wooden chair, lined up to match indentations made in the wall years ago, implicate someone who rocked too close. It might have been me.

The sky blue dust ruffle on my bed will brush my feet tonight as I get into bed.

I anticipate these details because now I see them only a few times a year. They remind me that no matter what happens anywhere else, here I'll find evidence that what I once was has been preserved.

I give Peter a kiss and he says, "Anne, this is Lisa." Lisa is tall, even an inch or two taller than Peter, and blonde. Aside from the black dress, everything on her matches—her lips, her earrings, her necklace, nails, and pumps.

"What a nice color," I say, trying to be friendly. "Is that what they call cranberry?"

"Puce," Lisa says, making two syllables of the word with her slight southern accent. She looks at me without letting go of Peter's hand.

"Can you believe I had to travel across the U.S. to find a girl who was, more or less, my neighbor?" Peter asks me. Lisa giggles and lowers her head.

Struggling out to meet me, Fam wags his tail slowly, almost in a circle, then lies down in front of me for a good scratching.

"He's getting up there," Peter says.

"Petie is going to get me a puppy," says Lisa. "Right, Petie?"

While Peter whispers to Lisa, Dad says, "That Fam. He fell asleep in my bowling bag one night last week." He looks at the dog and adds, "His eyes aren't so good anymore."

Mother interrupts Peter's explanation to Lisa that Fam is short for Family Man. "Neither is his bladder, Leroy," she says, still annoyed about the car horn, which I imagine has been added to their ragged list of arguments, repeated regularly, almost religiously.

Before I have my coat off, my mother says, "You take Peter's old room down here." In a lower voice she says, "Your brother wanted the big bed," and rolls her eyes toward Lisa as an explanation. She's referring to the double bed upstairs that used to be mine.

I stop in the bathroom and, after washing my face, pat it dry with the same blue towels I've used for years. I breathe in their familiar smell. When the towels wear out Mother buys the same colors again and again. Drying my hands, I think that what irritates me most is also what I value about returning—these assurances of stability that I find nowhere else in my life.

Peter's old room is the one with the twin bed covered with a wheat-colored blanket. Balling up clothes and stuffing them under the blankets, we once fashioned hills and moved our plastic men and horses over them. In that rugged, imaginary country, we always found something to fight about. As soon as I sit on the bed that Peter once slept in, I know something is different.

Looking carefully around the room, I see that someone else has been here, sleeps here still. The room even smells different. Colored bottles of aftershave and mouthwash, vials of medicines, line the top of the old walnut dresser in place of the clean space Peter left years ago. When I examine the shirts, hanging evidence of my father, in my brother's closet, I still don't understand.

"Come on, kids. Let's have something to eat," Mother calls.

"Mother," I say to her, pointing toward Peter's old room. Because I can't get her attention, I poke Peter, who is leading Lisa to a place at the table. "Your room's different," I tell him.

"So's yours," he answers. And I can't tell if he's trying to match me the way we did as kids or if what he says is true. Is the house itself finally altering, after years of constancy amid changes that have spread like forsythia?

"Oh that," says Mother when I bring up my discovery at the dinner table. She turns toward Dad. "There have been a few shifts." Looking at me, almost accusingly, my mother says, "You kids don't miss a trick."

Dad sticks his fork into a piece of meat, then lifts his head to look at it through his bifocals. "Got so I'd just fall asleep and Bette'd get into the bed. Then whoosh! I'd roll right into her." He laughs and makes a gesture for a landslide.

"It wasn't any picnic for me," says Mother, not smiling. "Leroy's up and down all night going to the bathroom."

"So, what's the setup? Dad sleeps in Peter's old room?" I say.

"And I sleep upstairs in yours. That way I can stay up sewing and run the machine all night if I want."

"Who sleeps in your old bed?" Lisa asks my parents. Lisa wants to know about the room on this floor on the other side of the bathroom, the room behind the closed door that was always out-of-bounds for Peter and me unless one of us happened to be sick. Now that room seems off-limits for my parents as well. There's a moment of silence, as if they're deciding who should tell her that the room's become a place from their past. But suddenly Mother says, "How about some more potatoes, Lisa." She's not asking a question.

After Lisa mentions something about high school, I don't have to do much calculating to figure she can't be older than nineteen, the same age as Peter's other wives when he married them. "Peter is the only one who gets any older," my mother had noted when she first called me about the sudden wedding. "If you can believe that," she'd said.

I watch my parents filling their plates. It's no wonder the sleeping arrangements have changed. Mother has grown to twice Dad's size; she's physically assumed a position of prominence. She notes who needs what on their plates and directs the serving dishes accordingly.

I want to ask my parents why they don't simply buy a new bed, a firm one that would at least solve my father's problem. But I know it's time to change the subject.

"How was Mary Beth's wedding?" I ask and take another spoonful of mashed potatoes.

"Didn't go," says Dad.

"You didn't? Mother talked about it for weeks. I thought you two were looking forward to seeing the relatives," I say.

"Well, it was supposed to snow. We didn't want to take a chance with treacherous weather," says Mother without looking up.

"It rained," says Dad. He passes me the pot roast. "Good luck for a wedding."

"Don't be so smart," Mother says. "Tell them what you told me," she says to Dad, then gestures in my direction. "You told me you'd rather watch the Orange Bowl than go to any old wedding. That's what you said," she accuses. Mother looks around the table for support. Dad shrugs his shoulders.

Out the dining room window, the parked cars are lit so brightly I guess the moon must be full. Then I bend forward and see only a streetlight, the moon nowhere to be found.

"Who wants coffee?" Mother hollers from the kitchen. I carry my plate and my father's out to the sink. "Doesn't your brother look thin?" she asks me. "He didn't say a word at dinner. He didn't stop eating to talk. He could use a little something to stick to his ribs."

"His ribs look OK to me," I say, but my mother ignores me.

"She never makes a decent meal. I'll put money on it." My mother never puts money on anything but women's magazines that feature new uses for leftovers. "This one probably doesn't get off her ass to answer the door." My mother refuses to use the word "Lisa," as if speaking the name will stamp approval on her son's marriage.

"Come on, Ma. Give the gal a chance."

"You still like the girls you room with?" she asks next, and I nod at her question. "Well, as long as you're happy."

"What's the holdup with the dessert, Bette?" Dad asks from the doorway.

"The maid took a break. She'll be right out," says Mother sarcastically. My father shakes his head and sticks a toothpick in his mouth. When he's out of sight she tells me I get "first crack."

"What are you talking about?" I ask.

She pours the steaming coffee and then looks at me. "Anything you really want you just let me know and I'll put your name on it. I can't stand the idea of that one running off with things I've had in the family for generations."

"You mean Lisa?"

"Shhh."

"Don't worry, Mom. If Peter lives up to his past record, Lisa will have a new name before you get arthritis."

My mother says, "I already have arthritis."

Her white hair smells of hair spray. "Do you still go to Mr. Carl's?" I think of the few times she dragged me to have my hair cut. As scissors clicked furiously, dangerously close to my face, I kept my eye on my mother, under the huge crown of a dryer. I knew she wouldn't hear me even if I screamed, "Ma, get me out of here."

"Carl still has the shop. I don't go once a week anymore. Just for special things." She slices into her homemade chocolate layer cake. "I looked like a million dollars for the Orange

Bowl," she says and shakes her head. "Leroy," she says in a sigh, then tells me that since he's been asked to think about retirement—as early as next year—he never wants to go anywhere but to Peter's old room to watch TV and to sleep. "It makes him confused staying cooped up in there all the time he's home."

After the dishes are washed and put away, Peter suggests we play a few hands of cards. "Oh, Petie, we can show them Casino," says Lisa brightening.

"No, not Casino, hon. I was thinking of poker." He takes her hand and puts it on top of his.

"Oh, why not? Cards is as good a way as any to kill an evening. Play some wedding songs in the background or something," says Dad.

Mother finds an FM station on the radio, while Dad hunts up his cache of pennies and makes change for all of us. I cover the dining room table with a plastic tablecloth.

When Peter says, "Anybody want a highball?" Lisa and I nod simultaneously.

Dad looks at Mother before he goes along. "Come on, Bette. For our son and our new daughter-in-law." He smiles at me. "And our daughter who's come all the way from Boston."

Peter makes the drinks and Dad directs me in angling the television until he can see it from where he sits. "Give a run through the channels as long as you're there," he calls.

"I thought you wanted music," says Mother, turning off the radio.

"Turn everything on," says Dad. "A real celebration."

"Dr. Pepper. Tens, twos, and fours are wild," says Peter. He whispers instructions to Lisa and then deals.

"Your mother tell you? Somebody else ran that stop sign at

the end of the street. That's the third time Al's had to repair his picket fence. I saw somebody run it at 6:30 one morning. I was on my way to work," says Dad. "It was when I knew I still had a job."

"Was anybody hurt?" I ask.

"Hurt? No. Nobody ever gets hurt. Old Al just has to repair his fence again. Been going on since you kids were babies." He looks around me at the television.

Suddenly Mother speaks up. She says, "Where could we move today? We sell this place, then where could we get a new house, any house, for $60,000 today?"

Nobody answers. We've all heard this concern of hers so many times that only Lisa looks in Mother's direction.

Peter asks if anyone wants another drink. "I'll get the ice," says Lisa. I picture Lisa checking out her eyelashes in the reflection of the toaster, the way I caught her earlier.

The cards are shuffled around the table again and again. Pennies clink and Mother does most of the winning. She pulls the pile of pennies toward her and says, "Well *I'm* in better shape than when I started."

"You got all my goddamn pennies," says Dad.

"You've had just about enough to drink," says Mother, looking around at all of us.

"Whose deal?" I ask and stare at Peter.

After a few more hands Mother says, "Well, I guess we can call it a night." Dad says something to counter Mother, while I direct Peter and Lisa upstairs. Lisa goes into my old room, leaving my brother just outside.

"What does she do in there?" I ask from the landing.

"She's taking off her makeup. Doesn't like me to watch." He quickly adds, "We've only been married five days."

"Not Lisa, silly," I say. "Bette. When we're not here. What does Ma do in there that she can't do downstairs?" I peek around him and through a crack in the door. What Mother said about sewing is confirmed by the piles of cloth in different colors, the calicos and tiny flowered patterns, the scissors and spools of thread neatly arranged in a corner of the room that once housed my stuffed animals.

"I don't get this whole arrangement. Them in our old beds. It's weird if you ask me," I say to him.

"What's to get? They don't sleep together anymore." Peter kisses me on the side of the head and gives my hair a tug like when I was his little sister.

From the top of the stairs I listen to my father in the kitchen as he readies the cups and coffee pot for morning. "Annie, come here, old buddy," he says, calling the dog by my name. But the dog understands; his nails scratch in response across the faded red and white linoleum.

When the lights go off downstairs and the double bolt slides into the locked position, I walk down to my brother's old room. Next door, my parents move around preparing for bed. I lie across Peter's bed, on top of the blanket that has always reminded me of a field of wild grasses. I wonder if anyone sleeps with someone their whole life. I wonder if from now on I'll sleep in a single bed instead of in a soft double like the one above me with the dust ruffle. The one that used to be mine.

Outside, the puddles of rain are freezing. The long, feathery branches of a neighbor's willow brush the icy surface, and then cannot pull away. With the plastic shade still up, the streetlight brightens the new objects in this room. My father's things—bottles on the dresser, the levels on all of them low; bowling and golf trophies that had been in storage the whole time I grew up; handgrips to strengthen hands that have grown softer and smaller; and a portable TV. Its blank face watches me until I close my eyes.

The first boy I loved lived one street over from this one. At night we climbed our neighbors' fences to reach each other. He climbed one; I climbed two. In total darkness we lay on the slope that was part of someone's backyard and made quick, hard love. Trying to forget about the fences containing our movements, I imagined us in a field. Tall grasses and far-off unending trees. And animals, hidden. The way this place had all been before any of us arrived. When we said good night, we each mounted a fence in a different direction.

Later, shortly before we broke up, he did favors for people or made deals so that we could use their beds. Once he bought a rifle for a guy who couldn't buy one for himself because of a criminal record. We got a water bed for two hours that night.

He never took me to a hotel.

In a real bed, everything was different. We expected more of each other.

Around me, the rooms, the furniture, are still the same, only now they've taken sides. In my mind I hear the sudden beginning notes of the song, "Bad, Bad Leroy Brown," announcing that something has changed.

Across the hall the toilet flushes and, in the room next to this one, the bed creaks and groans. Once again Bette and Leroy are in that bed for my sake and for Peter's.

All night my mother and father turn and turn in their old bed. The way animals circle a given spot before settling down to the ground.

Fortunes

Light after light appeared in small rooms throughout the neighborhood as evening settled against all the houses and grew thick and dark in each backyard. A car horn honked. Dolores and Pat, my mother's girlfriends, waited outside our house in the Vega.

"Come on and go with us, Carla," my mother said. "It'll do you good to get out."

"I don't know," I said. She'd been after me for about an hour to leave my room and stop "wallowing in self-pity." For most of my life, with the exception of the time I'd spent with Fred, she'd been trying to coax me from my small attic bedroom and into the world. As far back as I could remember she'd asked relentlessly, "Why don't you go outside and play?" as if sunlight and other children made you healthier than self-containment.

"Carla." When she set her purse on a chair by the door and pressed her lips together, I could see that if I didn't agree to go with her, she might not go herself.

Ever since I'd graduated from college the year before, my mother had made frequent attempts to include me in her activities. Sometimes, when I wasn't off with Fred, I obliged her. Like Fred, the neighborhood women were usually easy to talk to or to just sit with in silence. They knew most everything about me; my mother made sure of that. And they always had questions but without all the preliminaries, full of pauses groping at details, like when you meet someone new.

The car horn sounded again.

"Do I need to change?" I asked, staring down at my jeans and sweatshirt.

She didn't look at me, but motioned to the women from the front door. "You look fine. Let's go," she said, flashing the porch lights on and off, on and off. "Oh. Leave a note for your father."

"Where do I tell him we're going?"

"Just tell him that dinner's in the oven." While I carefully wrote on a napkin, my mother added, "Tell him shopping. Tell him we've gone shopping."

"I feel like I should be wearing lots of jewelry with stars and moons," I said to her back as she rushed down our three porch steps. "Or how about a big, full skirt?"

"Hi, gal," the women said to me simultaneously. One of them had overdone it with Shalimar. I slid across the backseat and my mother got in after me.

Pat stepped on the gas, and Sutter Road fell off behind us. We were on our way out of Baltimore to a place located just this side of Hagerstown, and which I knew only as "Nelly's." There, we would "get read," as Pat put it.

She lit a cigarette and then rolled down her window. The crisp June air rushed across my face. In another week or two, Baltimore would attract a thick veil of humidity, which would hold the summer in sticky immobility. Sometimes I felt it would be easy to let my mother and her friends spread their choices over me as naturally as weather. Other times, like now, I wanted to believe there was an alternative to the oppressive summers and icy winters.

Pat drove the back way, through the suburbs and small farms, as night came on and the women compared their grueling work weeks. Pat and Dolores and Estelle, my mother, designated Friday as a night away from "the boys." They preferred activities tinged with *the forbidden*, what they imagined might change their lives: a party where lingerie was sold, a nightclub where men stripped, a bingo game where the pot was over a thousand dollars, and tonight, Nelly's.

Pat had dyed black hair and a voice husky from smoking. "That Fred must be crazy," she said abruptly, glancing at me in the rearview mirror.

"A little down in the mouth is all," my mother said, explaining my silence.

In the next few moments when no one said anything, I realized that Pat knew all about my breakup with Fred Carter, my boyfriend for the past two years. Fred Carter. They'd invited me to come along because I was having "man troubles," as they put it. Such difficulties overrode our age differences and made me a member of their coterie.

"Nelly will set you straight," said Pat.

"Or bring her to her senses," Dolores said. Dolores shook her head of tight curls that reminded me of Raggedy Ann. Dolores smiled and used your name a lot when she spoke to you, and said "my good friend" before many people's names. Although my mother could never confirm this, Dolores's nearly constant grin gave me the feeling that before she'd moved to our neighborhood, she'd been shattered like a bisque doll, then stuck back together carefully, piece by piece.

"I've still got my senses," I said, unsure of my words even as I spoke them.

"Don't we all," said Pat, her wisecracking suddenly turning to resignation.

Pat was the only one who'd been to Nelly's before. All of us had heard the stories of Nelly's uncanny predictions and comforting advice, and the rumor that she'd once worked with the Baltimore City Police Department to locate a kidnapped delivery boy. "My sister-in-law swears by her," Pat said, her enthusiasm for the approaching adventure returning. "And Nelly's a hell of a lot cheaper than any psychiatrist."

Pat drove fast down the dark country roads and swirled around the bends. Once Dolores said, "Take it easy."

But Pat ignored her and said, "I told Jimmy I was going bowling tonight. The last time I went to Nelly's he gave me hell all week. Said I had an attitude problem."

Pat cut the lights on her car and drove gently, for the first time that night, into Nelly's large driveway, which led to a trailer and a separate garage. Gravel crunched under the tires.

"Oh shit," said Pat as she turned the ignition off and set her parking brake.

"What is it?" my mother asked anxiously. I realized she was unsure of what she was getting into, that she might not have gone on this trip at all if it hadn't been for me.

"I was hoping we'd be first," Pat answered. "There's three cars ahead of us."

Nelly did not make appointments. She took her clients one at a time, car by car, eight dollars per person.

"How many do you see in that station wagon?" Pat asked. Her plastic bracelets clacked together as she pointed.

My mother guessed four. "No wait a minute, five," she said.

"Five," I repeated.

"Damn," said Pat. She calculated that, at fifteen minutes a person, we had about a two-and-a-half-hour wait.

"Maybe they won't all go in," my mother suggested.

"They'll go in. Don't worry about that. Anybody that comes all the way up here and doesn't go in has something the matter with their head," Pat said. I patted my mother's damp hand. Two more cars pulled in, flanking us on either side.

At precisely nine o'clock, a porch light illuminated the outside of Nelly's trailer. It was old, worn in spots as if the elements had pressed too hard on it. The surrounding grass was high and loud with crickets.

"Here she comes," Pat said, lighting a cigarette. "Now we can get this show on the road."

At first, I thought a shadow extended around Nelly as she made her way slowly to the garage in front of which all of our cars were parked. But I realized my mistake when my mother said, "Will you look at the size of her." She spoke in a hushed tone, as if obesity in a fortune-teller demanded additional respect. As if each of Nelly's predictions had taken form and attached itself to her, her huge body proof of an ability to attract the unknown.

A light went on deep inside the garage. In the blackness the light was soft and hopeful, like the heart of something. Nelly waved for the first person in the first car to enter.

The parking lot was full.

"Hope you're hungry," Dolores said cheerfully. She unwrapped pieces of tinfoil, and the smell of fried chicken filled the car. As she passed around napkins and plastic forks, she explained that the utensils had been left over from a party at work. For a few minutes, the women gossiped about their coworkers. Dolores and Pat both worked for the Social Security Administration; my mother was a receptionist for three Baltimore County real estate lawyers.

Pat got out of the car, opened the trunk, and brought a cold six-pack into the front seat. "Estelle," she said, offering the first one to my mother. My mother never drank beer, but tonight she twisted the cap off without any help and put her mouth to the ice-cold bottle.

Drinking, I thought again of Fred and how he seldom went anywhere without a supply of beer. I gathered up images of driving with him to the movies, drinking and talking with him in his finished basement, swimming with him at Ocean City. At times I had almost begun to accept a predictable life in a few familiar places. Since we'd broken up, I felt as if I'd lost my place in a book, one that wasn't all that great, but that I still wanted to finish reading.

"Any problems, any questions, and Nelly will help you out," Pat reiterated.

"How's your studies going, Carla?" the women used to ask. Now that I was done with college and spent a lot of time filling notebooks with poems, the women didn't always know how to invite me into the conversation. They all wanted to know when I'd get a job worthy of my schooling. I worked nights as a cashier at the Super Giant supermarket and spent my days, at my mother's suggestion, sending out résumés and going on job interviews at public relations and marketing firms. I probably spent as much time considering graduate school as I did on my job search.

We sat in silence except for the crinkling of tinfoil and the gurgles of Budweiser bottles tilted to lipsticked mouths. All around us, women waited in dark cars with specific questions about their husbands, their lovers, their children. I had brought with me only a vague uneasiness that needed clarifying: I wanted some outsider to tell me what I looked like without a man, a boyfriend. Specifically, did I belong with the women around me, clutching disappointments as closely as their purses?

"That's one car down," my mother said. She'd been keeping track of people entering and leaving Nelly's garage. We were after the Ford truck. The relief I felt at forgetting about Fred for a time had been transformed into anxiety over what would soon happen, not between Fred and me, but between me and Nelly.

"Does she ever tell you tragic news?" I blurted out.

"Don't worry," said Pat, laughing, "you won't end up an old maid. Will she, Dolores?"

One by one, women entered and left Nelly's office, carrying their fortunes back to the others. The garage room seemed to breathe—exhaling light, inhaling darkness—each time the door opened and closed.

"I'm going to ask when my Susan's getting married," Dolores said while Pat was in with Nelly. Dolores had determined that we would have our futures told in the order of our ages. Pat was oldest by eight months.

"Shhh," my mother said, her superstition applying itself to the dark.

"It's OK to talk about what you're going to ask. Seriously," Dolores said. "It's not like when you make a wish or anything."

Comforted enough to pick up on the news of an impending marriage, my mother said, "I didn't know your daughter was engaged."

"She's not. But if Nelly can give me some particulars, like

what the fellow will look like, maybe I can speed things up." In Pat's absence, Dolores talked nonstop. Uneasy at being next, she kept her eye on Nelly's door and was out of the car the second Pat came into the light of the garage doorway.

My mother nervously, silently, prepared her questions. Catching her anxiety as if it were contagious, I tried to forget what lay ahead by talking to Pat.

"Unbelievable," Pat said. "I asked whether Jimmy's father would be moving in with us in the near future." Pat's father-in-law came into the Super Giant regularly and, for some reason, seldom used the express checkout aisle. He'd patiently stand behind someone with a full cart of groceries, as if he too were doing the week's shopping, although he had selected only a few items. Once I rang up a *TV Guide*, cat treats in a container the size and shape of a grade-school milk carton, and a pint of chocolate chip ice cream. He smiled at me and touched the three items, one by one, before I bagged them.

"That poor old coot," Pat said softly. "I don't know where we'll put him, though. Maybe we can make over the family room." Pat sighed and scratched her chin.

"Excuse me a minute," she said. She didn't go anywhere, but rooted in her purse for a pencil and began writing. "I always forget what Nelly's told me by the time I get home," she explained.

"She won't let you use a tape recorder?" I asked.

Pat shook her head.

"You don't know how good you've got it, Carla," Pat said. "No in-laws," she clarified.

"I'm not so sure," I said. Even in the dark, I could see Pat's eyes getting a little teary.

By the time my mother's turn arrived, her face was very

white. Her sweaty hands clenched mine, and she said she'd changed her mind. "Get your ass in there, Estelle. You're going to love it," Pat said.

I got out of the car with her and nudged her in the direction of the garage. "It'll be fine, Mom. Just don't ask what I got you for your birthday," I teased.

Pat lowered her window and said, "She's like my sister-in-law. After tonight, you won't be able to keep her away from here." Pat laughed.

I leaned up against the car and wondered what my mother would ask Nelly: about me without a boyfriend or any goals that she could understand, about my younger brother who drank too much, about the security of my father's job or the stability of their marriage? Would she reveal to a stranger the concern she'd only once expressed to me: that she might end up like *her* mother, falling asleep in the doorways of rooms, collecting house guests' watches at night, then putting them all on at once and asking which was her own? I wondered if my mother truly wanted to know about the unexpected events that were sure to change the direction of all of our lives, or if she only needed reassurance that everything would turn out all right.

Wide-eyed, my mother returned. She began talking quickly while still holding the handle to the Vega's back door. "She said I did something very rapidly that was a turning point in my life." My mother was referring to the story I'd heard since childhood: the crab picking contest she'd won in Crisfield, Maryland, on the Eastern Shore, where she'd grown up. At twenty, she had been the area's youngest winner.

"The crabs," she started to say, as if I could ever forget.

"How about marrying Pop?" I said in response. "That happened after a week, right?"

My mother put her hands on my shoulders and said, "Go," to assure me that I'd be healed by walking the dark length of driveway and talking to the fat woman who waited inside the garage.

Nelly's office did not look like a place where extrasensory things happened. There were no thick dark curtains, as I'd imagined while waiting in the dark car, or cats or candles or paraphernalia to coax the unseen into taking form. Nelly's garage looked like a garage, the walls lined with old newspapers and paint cans, a bicycle, a lawn mower, a rusted pair of shears. In the center of the space, a scarred rectangular table with two empty chairs awaited me. Nelly stood by one of them. Light emanated from a floor lamp with a cracked green shade positioned in one corner.

"Come in, come in," Nelly called invitingly. She lifted her large arm. The fat hanging on it shook as she motioned me in and pointed to an empty chair. She was about the age of the women who waited for me outside in the car.

"How about some coffee?" she said. I agreed tentatively.

"Have a seat, don't be shy," she said, her back to me as she measured the teaspoons of instant coffee and poured the water from a Hot Pot. I unfolded a five and three ones and pushed them toward her side of the table.

"Are you from New England?" she asked me as she set an orange place mat in front of each of us.

Although she hadn't read my palm yet, I thought she should be able to tell that I was my mother's daughter. This was how they got you. They asked simple questions under the guise of being chatty, having a cup of coffee, though I hadn't heard Pat or Dolores mention coffee. Then they put two and two together, as my mother would say. Maybe psychics were nothing more than perceptive women, tucked away in trailers, unable to use their intelligence in any other way.

"No," I said finally. I was remembering Vermont, camping with Fred shortly after we'd met. Fred had cooked eggs on a Coleman burner. Each time we opened our mouths as we ate, white clouds steamed out and floated up to match the early morning sky. We broke up at a Holiday Inn in Maine last week.

"You look like you're from New England," she said. I sensed her feeling me out. I was making the common mistake, the thing I accused everyone of who'd been to a psychic—*you bend whatever they say to fit your own life.*

Nelly must have picked up on my apprehension. She said, "This is strictly off the record, as they say. I haven't even had a look at you yet."

She delivered the steaming mugs of coffee to the table, and I was amazed at how gently such a big woman could take my hand. She turned it over and touched the creases and marks. Her softness made me strain with anticipation. What else would take me by surprise? She studied the side of my smallest finger for children. "Two," she said with confidence. And when I stared at her, she said, "You *will* have two." She said next that I'd had many many lives. "Or maybe experiences," she said, holding my hand and looking off.

At first, she told me things I had no way to dispute—that I'd have "female problems," that I'd marry in a church though I'd plan an outdoor wedding—and then facts that didn't seem very enlightening, that my parents worried about me, that I was a private person, a one-man woman, a creative individual, a person who didn't like to be corrected.

She held my hands together and asked me if I had any questions. I didn't want to inquire about my future with Fred, but I felt obligated, since everyone in the car outside would want to know. But before I'd spoken, she said, "Forget about the redhead. He's not worth the emotion you invest in him."

As if I'd been stung, I immediately looked at her straight on. She smiled subtly. I was amazed that she seemed to know me intimately, and at the same time, more objectively than I could see myself. My heartbeat quickened and I felt my hands begin to grow moist as my own mother's had a short while before. This was why the women came back to Nelly time after time. She was straightforward as no one else in their lives could be; she assured confused women that it was OK to leave their husbands or that it was perfectly honorable to take them back.

Nelly told me that I'd marry a man with the initials "B. W." "This is easy with someone who helps me," she said, smiling. I wasn't sure what she meant by that, and yet I was intrigued, seduced even, by the blunt way she referred to the details of my future.

"Hold on a second," she said. When she stood up, the metal chair stayed attached to her hips until she pushed it off. Her legs were the size of my file drawers.

"Your friends can wait a few extra minutes," she said, coming back with a pack of cards. Tarot cards.

I sensed then that Nelly could tell that I wouldn't be content with being told that everything would work out. Somehow she knew that I was curious about the specific surprises that add up to an individual life.

She shuffled the cards, which appeared to get lost in those thick fleshy hands. She was very intent as she set the cards out in a pattern and then turned them over. As she flipped each intricately designed card into view, she spoke. "You'll have two houses, one in the country and one, like a town house, in the city."

She flipped more cards. "You'll never compete with other women for your husband's love, only with his work." She looked up at me. Her eyes were small and very blue in her puffy face. "You'll work but you won't have to." I thought of the women in the car, every day exhausted by work and traffic and then having to cook and tend to a family.

What she told me was what I'd been waiting to hear: it was OK for me to take on a different life.

The revelations came first like raindrops developing into a fine mist, then an outburst. I tilted my head back and allowed everything she said to touch me.

"You'll see forty-seven of the fifty states and travel to Europe and the Caribbean and Australia."

I always knew I didn't belong to the place where I'd been born. One night at Fred's after we'd drunk rum and Cokes for hours with friends, someone said from out of nowhere, "I wonder what will happen to us." And someone else, it might have been Fred trying to be funny, said, "We'll probably turn out just like our parents." Nobody laughed.

"You'll be successful as an artist," Nelly said. She looked up. "It's either words or architecture that you're gifted in. I'm not sure which."

She turned the final card, lifted it and showed it to me as proof of everything she'd said.

"The world," she said softly, with reverence. "This is the highest of the cards." Her eyes were soft and damp with amazement.

What she told me carried me far from the white shingled house on Sutter Road in Baltimore, where I'd grown up. Where people worked hard on weekdays, and cut their grass and waxed their cars on weekends. And watched one another's children grow.

Nelly had given me a gift I wasn't supposed to open for some years to come. But already I knew what was inside. It was much bigger than any news about a boyfriend. Nelly was permitting me, inviting me even, to proceed with my life without a precedent. That prospect was both exciting and frightening; no one I knew could help me. I wished for this special life and didn't wish it, and yet, as Nelly spoke, I knew all she had said would come true.

Walking out to the car I felt as if I'd overdressed for an occasion I'd mistaken for formal. The sensation reminded me of a dream I frequently had, in which everyone was in acceptable pants and nice blouses and I'd shown up wearing velvet—a strapless black gown.

As soon as I was in the car, Dolores handed me a piece of paper. I thanked her, but I didn't have to write anything down. I remembered Nelly's words precisely.

"Well, Carla, cat got your tongue?" Pat asked, starting the car.

"She had you in there long enough," Dolores said. Her voice was muffled by a napkin as she wiped her mouth of chicken grease.

"Are you and Fred getting back together?" my mother asked gently. My mother liked Fred. He had a good job with General Electric, benefits that included dental. He got me out of my room. And she'd started him on a collection of beer mugs, which she had presented at each Christmas and birthday.

I shook my head and let them think I wanted to be alone with my love life. I knew they'd be understanding of that.

"Be careful pulling out of here, Pat," my mother advised. "Kids drinking on a Friday night could come around this corner—"

Stepping on the gas, Pat cut my mother off. My mother put one hand to her throat, the other on my arm.

"Nelly didn't say anything about an accident to me. You Dolores?" Pat asked and laughed. Gravel sprayed in pings against the car. I knew what her husband must have meant about Pat's attitude once she'd been with Nelly. Pat felt impervious to any disaster, even to her father-in-law's moving into her house.

"Well, does everybody feel better?" Dolores asked, looking right at me.

"My Jimmy's never going to believe I bowled this long," said Pat, smiling and glancing at her watch.

I rolled the window down a few inches. The cool breeze caught my hair and tossed it back. I felt lifted up, my life to this point dropping away as smoothly as my clothes soon would. With the summer air cool on my flushed face, I was certain I'd not be among them for long.

As we drove back toward our houses, with their rooms now lit like many moons in a black night, I listened to the women chatter about how much Nelly made off the books, and about a neighbor's husband who'd come home late every night for a week, and then about a good recipe for ground turkey. I closed my eyes and before long their voices chattered together like birds welcoming another day.

Dogs

I dreamed my grandmother's dog was alive. I stroked the animal's head, his hair matted and shiny from so many old hands, until he gave a slight whine. His eyes lowered as if he were once more enduring being dressed up in a hat or shirt that belonged to one of my dolls.

In the dream, I said, "God, he must be thirty years old." And I was prepared, anxious even, to take Snooks home and care for him, simply because he was a part of my grandmother. On waking, I immediately realized that Snooks would be far older than thirty. My grandmother outlived all her dogs, and she had died twenty-five years ago.

The dream was not uninspired. Yesterday one of my father's two dogs had been destroyed. "It's over," my brother, Peter, said when he called from his apartment in Baltimore, about twenty minutes from our parents' home.

"What?" I asked, although I knew what he meant. We'd been talking about the fate of Dad's favorite dog for weeks. I was on my way to an audition halfway across town from my apartment in New York, but I sat down and listened to Peter.

"We had Phony put to sleep yesterday," he said, his euphemism echoing Mother's stand-in phrase for death—"if something happens."

When Peter and I were growing up, I'm sure Mother believed a dog was as replaceable as any of the fuzzy-haired dolls lining my bed. When I cried over one of them—Lady's ear infection, Fam's condition after he'd eaten an entire coffee can full of assorted greases—Mother tried to assure me that we could always get another dog "if something happens."

Before I could respond to Peter's announcement, he went on, "There wasn't anything else we could do," and then he was quiet.

"How's Dad?" Four years earlier our father, at seventy-two had been forced to retire from the Baltimore Gas and Electric Company where he'd worked for forty-five years. At his retirement dinner, the company presented him with a bowling ball engraved with his name and the date of retirement. Not long after that, Dad gave up bowling and retreated into a state of general bewilderment. Lately, he mixed up names and dates and times of day, even calling our mother by the name of a girlfriend from his youth.

"He's OK." After a pause Peter said, "I hope I did the right thing."

I wasn't sure that he had, and yet I could tell he needed reassuring. During the past year, the small brown and white mutt had scratched most of the fur off her front legs and hind quarters. Whenever Phony went outside, she rubbed herself back and forth, back and forth, against the aluminum fence that squared off our tiny backyard, until Dad dragged her back inside. He tried to discourage Phony's habit by wrapping her legs with heavy packing tape, but she always managed to bite the tape off.

The vet and nearby pet shop recommended a number of salves and shampoos, none of which alleviated Phony's condition for more than half a day. Lola, Peter's girlfriend, suggested that the dog's problem was psychological, stress induced, and Peter passed the diagnosis on to Dad. When Lola went on about dog psychiatrists and the trauma Phony might have suffered when a second dog, Java, moved into the house, Dad ran his hand against his chin or shook his head in confusion. I thought if he kept up the rubbing, his chin would end up as raw as Phony's legs and hairless tail.

Peter explained how he'd held the miserable dog as the vet injected the death potion. "Anne," he said, "I pretended Phony wasn't Dad's." I heard him take a deep breath. Then in a stream of words, he said, "I was embarrassed bringing this hairless dog into the office so I told the vet that Phony belonged to an old man who lived down the street. I said I didn't even know the dog's name. And then right before the vet, you know, the dog looked at me, and I lost it. I said, 'Persephone, it'll be all right.'"

"At least Dad still has Java," I said quickly. My brother's admission stunned and implicated me. Both Java and Phony had originally belonged to me. But, due to circumstances involving men, I hadn't been able to keep either of them.

I bought Persephone for ten dollars when my college boyfriend and I were in the process of rejecting each other. Fearing that Carl's memories of me would center on dope smoking and staring into his fifty-gallon aquarium, I presented the puppy to him as a symbol of the brief time he had loved me simply because I relied on him.

"What's its name again?" Carl had asked me.

He returned the puppy to me two weeks later, and the following week, in his car redolent of greasy hamburgers and fries, we said good-bye. In spite of Carl's warnings that Persephone couldn't be housebroken ("Some dogs just don't learn"), I talked to the puppy, walked her, and trained her within a week. Being unattached gave me a dedication to persistence.

Even my mother was impressed with the dog's obedience. Although she said, "We'll keep her only until you find a good home for her," I knew that the pet's welcome at home was dependent on my own willingness to continue living there.

Instead of nicknaming the dog Perse or Seph, Dad called her Phony and always laughed when he revealed the name to people. "Where's that Phony?" he'd ask. The dog would almost laugh, too, pulling her lips over her teeth in a weird grimace.

I soon got a job with a newspaper in Providence and an apartment where the landlord allowed pets of no kind. "Not even turtles," he told me in a half whisper, as if he were revealing confidential information.

"And just what are we going to do with *your* dog?" Mother asked, before congratulating me on my new job.

"Well, Dad—" I started to say.

"Dad nothing. This is *your* dog." But the dog stayed with my parents. Maybe my mother thought Phony would lure me home for holidays, which I might otherwise spend with new friends. Or maybe she recognized what she couldn't understand—the easy way that Dad and Phony exchanged affection. Dad had been without a dog for two months, ever since Fam, on one of his brief escapades, had chased a Pontiac exactly like Dad's into deadly traffic.

Java was the second dog I bequeathed to my father, after another relationship dissolved. The week Jeremy and I moved in together, we selected Java from a litter of liver and white springer spaniels. The breeder's kitchen full of puppies and formulas and the long list of family dog names, some highlighted to indicate a champion, was so impressive that, for a while, Jeremy and I considered breeding dogs ourselves. But before Java went into her first heat, Jeremy found a genuine mission in the Peace Corps. I moved from our rented house in Vermont to a studio in New York City and took Java with me.

When I'd return home from my job at the Broadway ticket office, where all day I assigned show seats to callers identifying themselves with credit card numbers and expiration dates, I attempted to walk Java. Not used to sidewalks and city commotion, Java tucked under her trembling, stubby tail, bent her legs, and lowered her head; she appeared to crawl down the street. She seldom made it to the park. Sometimes a stream appeared as she slunk along, involuntarily emitted when the backfiring of a truck or the blowing of a whistle startled her. Most often we returned home to the sixth floor where, on the familiar hardwood floor of the studio, Java would relieve herself.

"No more dogs," my mother said when I first explained this tortuous ritual. She said "dogs" to me as firmly as she said "beer" to my brother or "cigars" to my father.

"What else can I do?" I asked, pleading.

"I don't know. Your father's retiring."

"What does that have to do with it? Besides, he'll need something to do. He could use two dogs."

"And I'll end up taking care of all three of them," Mother said.

"Ma, you've never had to take care of the dogs." She allowed Dad one household responsibility—caring for the family dogs. Whenever Mother corrected me or Peter, whether dealing out threats or physical blows, Dad made his escape. After he slipped out of the house to walk the dog around the block, I pictured the pet alternately pulling hard against its lead and retching from the pressure at its throat.

"Now it's different," she said, a new worry covering her voice. Dad was significantly older, she reiterated to me in a hushed tone, and she feared that once he stopped working, he'd quit doing anything dependable.

Peter offered to adopt Java. But after two months of no better luck than I, he delivered Java to Dad. Peter had coerced Mother by saying that Dad needed a backup dog. Mother said while Peter was at it, he could get himself a backup job. They argued briefly and then made up, he eating third helpings of her chicken dinner and she adjusting and readjusting the paper napkin on her lap while gently saying to her son, "You're no different than when you were ten years old."

My brother called me with weekly reports of Java's strange reactions to Phony's absence. Java had begun to snap at Dad when he dangled his hand over the side of the den's recliner. She refused to leave the house except for once every morning when she made one quick round through the backyard, probably as much to check for signs of Phony as to relieve herself. Other times she balked at the door and was impervious to Mother's foot or to Dad's coaxing with meaty treats. The dog planted herself in the spot between the kitchen and basement doors that had always been Phony's and refused to budge.

Mother called Java an odd dog, one that would "turn on you" for no apparent reason, and closed the kitchen door whenever a neighbor stopped by to visit. Eventually Java refused to allow Dad up or down the cellar stairs. She growled and lurched when anyone touched either one of the door handles.

My brother took Java away the same way he'd coaxed

Phony—with a soft low voice and promises only a dog could understand. It was hard to imagine that the boy who'd once made a saddle for our collie and attempted to ride him down the back steps had developed such a tenderness for animals in distress.

"I didn't tell Dad," Peter said to me.

"What do you mean?" I asked. The traffic below my apartment was loud and yellow with rush-hour cabs.

"I didn't say I had Java put to sleep. I said I gave her to a guy who has a farm where she could run."

I thought of how, far from the city, farms could still sound like magical places where anything could be cured, anyone enlightened.

Peter had gone to a different vet this time, one who didn't ask the dog's name. And this time Peter didn't witness the death but waited outside. The vet said it had taken a muzzle and three injections to "put the dog down."

"Never again," Peter said to me, his tone humbling me.

Dad had been tearful when Phony was taken from the house, but when he looked at Java's empty bowl, he began to mourn openly.

My mother phoned at two o'clock in the morning. "You won't believe it. He's crying like it's a person that passed away."

"He wants to go see Java at 'the farm.' What am I going to do?" she asked another time.

"He says *I* made your brother get rid of Phony." My mother recited the accusation with hurt coloring her voice. "He says I never liked any of the dogs. From the beginning."

"He's going crazy on me, Annie."

When Peter and I were growing up, my mother didn't hate dogs, but she referred to them as things that got in her way, like slow-moving traffic, like the stack of textbooks and notebook pages on the kitchen table just before dinnertime. She considered dogs as property that came with marriage and a family, or like the packet of turkey giblets, which she never liked touching but never eliminated from the gravy. But for a woman who repeated, "It's only a dog" whenever I showed unwarranted sympathy for one of them, she had always handled their "close calls" with seriousness.

If the gate in the chain-link fence had been left open when she pushed a dog out the kitchen door and in the direction of the yard, the docile animal would become a wild beast at the possibility of freedom. And when the pet escaped, Mother would hold the kitchen door open, uncharacteristically extravagant with the heat, and scream, "THERE HE GOES." Then she gave orders. Peter and I were not to leave our post at the open gate, while Dad was to drive the car around the neighborhood. Later, as the dog panted furiously against the kitchen wall, Mother chastised the adventurer. And when she finally had a cigarette, her hands shook. It was the same worry she showed when my brother and I went off to college, or even to the corner store by ourselves. Released to the world, out of sight of her domain, we must have seemed like crazed animals ourselves, in pursuit of independence from the place she'd made for us.

Dad was seventy-six. Without his dogs or his job, he was a man without a place of his own. The only thing I could think to do for my father—despite my mother's threat, "NO MORE DOGS" and my brother's "Never again"—was to give Dad a puppy for his birthday.

My mother didn't put up the resistance I'd anticipated when

I brought the tiny half bulldog, half terrier into the house. She was too preoccupied with the melancholia that often took away my father's voice, as well as his appetite. "He doesn't want to eat." "I only do one load of laundry a week now." "I have to tell him to change his clothes," she whispered to me at intervals. She feared she was becoming as useless to him as he had become to the world.

She was also interested in the guarantee that came with my gift. I, who seldom spent more than a night away from New York, promised to stay in Baltimore for as long as it took to train Princess Gina, which was the name my father gave the puppy. From the look my mother shot him, I got the feeling that Gina was some old secret he no longer cared to hide.

I suspected my parents once had an unspoken agreement—that when Peter and I were on our own, there would be no more pets, no more responsibilities for either Mother or Dad. But since my brother and I now had unpredictable lives (frequently he paid his rent only after a successful day at the track), Mother must have considered that at any time one or both of us could end up back at the house.

By morning the dog's name had been shortened to Princess, and she sat her chubby black and brown body on my father's chest as he lay in bed. Her hair was short and shiny, her triangles of ears pricked up at the slightest sound.

I woke up several times each night to carry the baby dog from its plastic laundry-basket bed behind the kitchen door, down the back stairs and outside. After the first couple of times, Princess would wet wherever I set her down, and then I'd praise her. If she bounded off into the blackness, a slight whistle from me would bring her back with her cigar of a tail beating, her legs trembling with cold.

My mother often followed me outside in the dark. She confided her fears: "You should just take it back with you. We're too old for a puppy." But I ignored her the way I'd once disregarded any advice that began, "You're too young to . . ." I could tell that she needed to scold me again. Dad, she said, was as responsive as a mummy these days.

The puppy was housebroken in ten days. She would wait by the hinged side of the door and whine until my father or I carried her down the steps to the closely cropped grass where she would immediately squat.

"I'll be damned," my father said, amazed at the successful toilet training. "Princess," he called, snapping fingers that seemed to be shrinking into themselves, the outer skin hanging slack. The puppy yelped and returned to his open hands. "Let's feed her," he suggested.

At dinner my father stopped wiping his eyes and finished everything Mother put on his plate. Soon Mother returned to humming in the kitchen. I took the train back to New York, but my brother called our parents or stopped by every other day to see how Princess was progressing.

Weekly conversations with my mother were full of news about Princess—her shots and wormings, then her appetite. Gradually, details became more descriptive—"Her tongue looks as long as a fork. Is a dog's tongue supposed to be that long?"

Dad picked up the extension phone. "Your mother got Princess to sit today. That dog is smart as a whip." I smiled at the thought of them playing with Princess, as my cat wound possessively back and forth through my calves.

One day my mother shocked me when she called to say, "I just don't know what's wrong with our little Princess. She didn't touch her hamburger."

This was the same woman who'd once reassured me that if Lady didn't survive her faulty rabies shot we could get another dog the very next day. Maybe the dogs had been more important to her than I'd ever realized, and by acting unaffected, she'd only been trying to protect me and Peter from future pain. More likely she was coming to see what I'd known all along—how dogs held our fiercest emotions and dispensed them like time-release vitamins.

I talked to my brother on the phone about the change. He said, "Ma practically runs after that dog with a roll of toilet paper." Laughing, maybe out of relief that he could once again say the word "dog" without feeling intense guilt, Peter said, "It even has a goddamn jogging suit."

Because I'd been on the road in a show, I hadn't visited my parents' house in seven months. Dad greeted me with a quick hug and said, "Look at Princess coming to greet you."

Standing beside me, Peter seemed not to notice that the young dog's stocky legs hardly held its stomach off the carpeted floor. Princess looked like a cartoon, with her large head and long tongue and stumps for legs. I was amazed that she was allowed the run of the entire house.

"So," said Dad, "how's show business?"

"It's fine," I answered, still looking at the dog. "We have two final shows in Philadelphia next week."

"What then?" Mother asked.

"Then I look for work again."

"Me too," Peter said, explaining that he'd just completed an eight-week job as a driver for the crew of a movie shoot in Baltimore. Peter went on about the actors he'd met and the amazing speed with which the set artists painted signs.

Normally my brother's movie stories would have fascinated me, but I was distracted by the dog. In my absence, a phenomenal change had taken place. Instead of just filling a void in my father's routine, Princess led my parents back to their early years when Mother took domestic charge, dishing out caring in second helpings, and my father replicated her duties with his dogs.

But now dinner conversation was no longer the old clash between the outer world of my father's dealings with faulty gas lines and new wiring and the domestic territory of Mother's broken dishes and the children's stomach aches. During meals my parents discussed what had evolved into common ground—Princess.

Mother served the dog a plate of each thing we had, chopping the meat and potatoes and vegetables into bite-size pieces as she'd once cut mine and Peter's. Ignoring Mother's special preparations, Dad picked a select piece of meat from his plate, lowered his hand down the side of his chair, then wiggled the morsel to catch Princess's attention.

We'd just about finished eating, but Princess was begging for seconds. Without looking up from his plate, Dad said, "Don't forget to cut it up."

Mother was talking seriously about her will, about a rider involving Princess. She was asking me something, but I couldn't concentrate on her words, only on the dog slurping below me.

The dog panted and wheezed as if it had just gotten back from an escape around the block, but it had merely finished eating. I worried that the dog, with its bulging eyes and its long dripping tongue, would outlive both my parents.

After dessert I pushed back from the table and explained that I wanted to return to New York before it got too late.

"Well, we've hardly talked to you," Mother said.

"You just got here," Dad added.

I stared at the monstrous dog looking at me. This was what could become of someone who never left this house, this neighborhood, this town. Overfed, barely able to move, and yet, somehow, quite effortlessly, bringing purpose into two aging lives. And while it sickened me, I was thankful for the dog, for all the animals that I had entrusted with some of my hardest jobs.

By the time I left the old house, I was thinking of how even the single syllable—"dog"—was complex. When I was a girl and my mother and father fought and she called him a dog, the hard beginning of the word and the dull clanging of its ending were spat with anger through her lips. Other times, when he teased her into giggling, she called him a dog again. But in those happier instances, the noun sounded like an entirely different word—long, drawn out, slightly southern-accented, and unhampered by hard consonants. I couldn't hear the word "dog" without seeing a long line of pets, stretching all the way back through my childhood. They bent to what would please us, were burdened with our intentions. We invested in them all the secrets we could never speak among ourselves.

Visiting Hours

*W*eekends after graduation from college, I drank Colt 45 with Tommy Fortuno and drove long and fast into the night in his secondhand '67 Triumph. Old Route 209. We drove as if we were really on our way somewhere. But somehow we always woke up on Monday morning in our separate beds, and went off sleepily to our separate jobs. Weekdays, between 7:30 and 8:45 A.M., I wrote obituaries for Scranton's daily newspaper.

At my deadline I'd turn in the collection of abbreviated life stories. As they were read and approved by the city desk, I'd smoke my first cigarette and finally say good morning to a few reporters. While I began more leisurely to write church news or club notices or food stories, on the floor below me the obituaries were transformed into type, then arranged and stuck in place on pages that would appear at the back of the second section—local news—in a couple of hours.

My other stories didn't turn up for days, weeks. Though these accounts took up three quarters of my day, it was the obits I was known for; it was the obits I had to be most careful with. And when people outside asked me what I did at the paper, "Obituaries" was my immediate response. That made them giggle or shift all their weight onto one foot, or the bolder ones to say, "Oh, come on." Their reaction was partly my fault; I always made "obituaries" sound like the punchline to a joke.

That year I was twenty-one, and my mother still asked me not to laugh with food in my mouth. One morning on my way to the paper, a morning before I recognized that her tightly curled, newly darkened hair was a sign of her aging, she said, "Don't you and Tommy ever talk about anything serious? You know what I'm talking about."

As the screen door slammed behind me and I walked toward my Volkswagen parked tight against the curb, my father called, "Hey, when's the last time you checked the oil in that thing?" The question was rhetorical. He checked mine every time he checked his own. Though I didn't turn around, I knew they both stood together in silence. Her hands held open on her full hips; his fingers deep in pockets, where they moved the coins into a jingle that irritated her. I believed then what they both denied—there was all the time in the world.

I also believed that in one small way I was an accomplice in the responsible world that was just beginning to lay claim all around me. I never made a mistake with a person's name. Time after time I'd report the wrong date of a firemen's carnival or a mother's club bake sale, or type something like three tablespoons of salt when the recipe called for teaspoons. But I never misspelled a name. I was meticulous with the names the undertakers or funeral directors would speak, then spell to me, seconds after I'd gotten out of my jacket and turned on the typewriter.

If my nights with Tommy Fortuno were careless flights of fantasy, my mornings spent on the phone with undertakers were a formula, fitted to different names and details. Facts were read to me with dull precision. "Mrs. Lydia Candell, seventy-three, a resident of this community for the last twenty-nine years, died yesterday at Irvington Memorial Hospital after a long illness." Death was either the result of a long illness or a short illness, or it was termed accidental. The precise cause of death never sullied the obit, which would find its way into Bibles and scrapbooks, or through the mail slots and into the mailboxes of distant relations, as well as into the bottoms of wastebaskets, onto high, damp basement piles, and, as Tommy once reminded me, under dog piss.

The second, usually brief, paragraph recounted the deceased's career and affiliations—Elks Lodge, the Altar Guild at church, the Veterans of Foreign Wars. In the list of survivors that followed, my attention to names was paramount. One slipup and five or six angry—or worse, tearful—relatives might call to complain; a family wound stitched tenuously closed for years might reopen. The soft, fleshy face of the city editor warned me of this possibility the day I took the job. He ran his fingers across his head, lingered at the few places where his hair remained an afterthought. He compared my position to a cop's on a domestic-violence call. "You can't afford to be too careful. One misspelling—even a single letter—and all hell can break loose."

After I'd finished that section as cautiously as if weaving through road construction, the funeral home representative would finally read the line I'd waited for since the start, the cue that we were on the final paragraph of the obituary. "Visiting hours will be two to four and seven to nine tonight, at . . ." Then he would supply a name and address. Usually this was his funeral home, though sometimes a family arranged for traditional visitation at the house of the deceased.

Wherever visiting hours were held, they were what people

looked for as soon as they recognized someone in an obit. The readers needed to know the appropriate time to pay their respects, the city editor emphasized. He also said that "visiting hours," not "viewing," was the paper's accepted terminology. Only one line, combining funeral and burial arrangements, followed the information on visiting hours. Then I'd read back the nearly two-page account that had taken six or seven minutes to type as if it were privileged information, a secret between the two of us, not an announcement about to reach thirty-some thousand readers. I'd hang up the phone, which would ring again immediately. Well warned of my deadline, my mother waited until after ten o'clock to call with suggestions for dinner or questions about my short-range plans. And Tommy never called me at work. For my first hour and fifteen minutes on the job, I talked only with people representing families of the deceased.

By the end of the summer, every undertaker in town and a few long distance knew my name. They respected my attention to middle initials, as well as to Greek and Polish surnames as long as pencils. The first time my own family's name showed up in an obituary, Peter Rose, of Rose Funeral Home, spoke it as carefully as if he'd just eaten something too hot. Then he said, "These people wouldn't be any kin to you, would they?" I reassured him that my extended family lived in Virginia. Then it was OK to joke. "Some string of kids. No wonder he didn't belong to anything like the Moose Club. No time for outside activities." At the emphasis on the word "outside," I realized that if Tommy had been listening he would have rolled his eyes. He hated small talk, especially when people tried to manipulate it into a joke.

Heeding the number of obituaries I had to complete by my

deadline, the undertakers kept their chatter to a few light remarks, just to get me through the routine. Not one of the funeral directors ever confided what a widow looked like, if a certain body was difficult to reassemble and paint with life, if the deceased seemed well loved. And I never asked.

Every obituary and filler I wrote, every story the other reporters completed, was scanned by the city desk before being typeset. The desk never called me on a misspelling; they trusted my accuracy. The editors were most concerned with my speed. They wanted each obituary that had been phoned in before 8:45 to appear in print by 11:00 A.M. The obituary page, along with the main page of local news, and the front page of the paper were designated "live pages," which meant they could be changed and added to at the last minute.

The other reporters ignored my frenzy about meeting a deadline. They wanted to reach their own without the interruption of a stray obituary I might be too busy to handle. Even if one of the calls was directed elsewhere, it usually came back to me; most of the funeral directors preferred dangling on hold to taking a chance with accuracy.

What did interest the other reporters, and what concerned the city desk maybe more than my making that deadline, were the sudden deaths—the suicides, the accidents, the dead young—which might quietly and curiously bypass police reports and come to me first. My mention of "accidentally" flagged the editors. Between my routine sentences, the city editor searched for potential page one headlines—a car sliced in half on impact the night of the senior prom, a man electrocuted while trimming the willow in his front yard, an unpredicted leap from the roof of the only twenty-story building in town. I never wrote these stories. A beat reporter stalked the funeral director, the hospital, the family for enough details to form a picture. I had only to say "died accidentally" in the obituary, and then forget about it.

I seldom shared the gruesome accounts, or even routine ones, with Tommy. Oh, once I made him laugh, when I mimicked Mr. Leggitt, of Legg Funeral Home, who'd called drunk at eight o'clock in the morning and mumbled the names as if he spoke from under water. I didn't tell Tommy how carefully I caught and saved each name as if picking up beads from a broken strand. And I didn't tell him that no one had ever called with a complaint. Tommy didn't generally talk about his father's construction company either. His summer job there, like our weekends together in the old Triumph, had somehow begun to feel permanent.

I only remember once that he mentioned his work. The beginning of November we parked a half mile from the state park. We walked to it, and crept over and beyond the wooden gate that had been locked since Labor Day. Tommy carried a bottle of cheap champagne and two hard plastic glasses. We sat in the snow by the side of the lake and drank champagne, and for a long while nothing around us moved.

Tommy pushed back his black ski cap, just about the color of his eyes, and said, "I hate like shit to work for him." Then he took off his gloves, took my face in his hands, and kissed me hard. I looked into the sky gray with the inevitable—more snow. I watched his breath match the color of the sky.

Every once in a while a bird would light in a tree, then become part of the tree, part of a cluster of sharp branches. I thought of all the things Tommy and I didn't talk about. Before we got back to the car it was snowing. He reached behind the car seat for another bottle. When the plastic stopper hit the roof, we laughed and drove into what became blackness. Tommy finally turned on his headlights and said, "What do you say we head for Florida? I've never been to Florida." I don't remember which of us decided to turn around, but I guess that it was me. Even then I must have known that Florida wasn't far enough.

As the weather became colder, as the nights grew longer and the snow deeper, as I wrote obituary after obituary, something changed. When I think of those long bony fingers on the winter trees, I think maybe they were pointing to the end of something.

The morning of Christmas Eve I still hadn't gotten Tommy a present. And when I walked to my desk at the newspaper, I put off worrying about it once again, because my phone was already ringing with an obituary. Many of the funeral directors had more than one to give me that morning. They all said in one way or another, "It's sad, but this is our busiest time of year." As I quickly fed page after white page into my typewriter and darkened them all with words, the city editor, whose advice I never got around to testing, tapped my shoulder and said, "Springtime. Just wait. You won't believe the number of suicides in springtime."

I took each story of a death and accepted the Merry Christmas that concluded each conversation. I was still typing with three calls on hold at 9:00. The deadline was moved to 9:15, then to 9:30, finally to whenever I finished. The paper came out an hour and a half late, at 12:30. Every filler, every announcement of a library's holiday hours, every New Year's workshop to stop smoking and clinic to lose weight, every recipe for egg nog and holiday appetizers had been scrapped to make room for the obituaries.

I glanced quickly in amazement at the pages of obituaries, then went on to the store ads to get an idea of what to buy Tommy. I flipped past page after page of dress shirts, beer mugs that belonged in glass cupboards, initialed belts, and expensive colognes. I sighed at the thought of stopping after work. Old Route 209 would be packed with cars that time of day.

Then he got off the elevator. Tall and thin and wearing a long black coat, he looked like an exotic bird. Someone pointed out my desk. He introduced himself as Harvey Smithson, of Smithson and Sons Funeral Home. Looking down, he peeled off one glove and awkwardly shook my hand. His hand was not cold, but the fingernails were yellowed as old smoker's teeth. Then with this same hand he quickly, smoothly, ran his fingers along the length of my wooden desk. It was a gesture I knew he practiced every day at work. A tremor startled me as if he were running his fingers down my spine. Only then did I notice the coffin shape and size of the desk before me. We looked at each other but I could say nothing. He reached into his front coat pocket and pulled out an envelope I later found held twenty dollars and Christmas wishes.

For the rest of the afternoon, other funeral directors came with cards and gifts of appreciation. They drifted to my desk as a reminder of every name I had ever spelled right. They thanked me for the good and careful job I'd done. Their procession of suits and coats was darker than any conglomeration of words I'd written so far. Instead of money, a couple of them presented me with gifts—a box of chocolates, a basket of fruit. One of them set flowers before me.

Sign

At first, right after the accident, Sam visited Amy every day. But since August he's gone to her quiet room, her immovable body, the purr of machinery replacing her voice, only once a week.

Sam can't imagine having time every day to drive from Union Memorial Hospital in Baltimore back home to Hampstead. To save himself an extra trip, on the last three visits he's driven directly from work to the hospital. Since he's been pouring concrete for a builder in Baltimore all month, this arrangement makes sense. The only problem is that Sam doesn't have a chance to shower first, so he arrives dusty and disheveled at the hospital, as if he, not his wife, had been in the accident. Even so, Sam looks healthy, and his thirty-five-year-old face is almost boyish with its wide-set eyes and sandy-colored hair that doesn't show a sign of gray.

The nurse, who must be in her fifties—Joan, he's heard one of the younger nurses call her—says, "What you got there, cutie?" as he walks to Amy's room. She must mean the bag. Sam just nods and keeps walking. By now he knows his way down the shiny white and green corridors; he doesn't have to stop and endure scrutiny at the nurses' station. He sets the bag down and slaps his palms against his jeans before touching the door to Amy's room, the way he does at work before he opens his lunch pail.

Sam stares at Amy's closed eyes. They resemble perfect shells, hard and just out of reach. Pieces of some lovely sculpture not part of his world. Even when he bends and kisses her lightly on the forehead, then the lips, her lids don't flutter. Where he's touched her face, tiny particles of cement dust remain. But when he stands back from her, she looks flawless and light. She appears younger than thirty-one.

Before the accident, Amy worked as a secretary for the Social Security Administration, where she received total medical benefits. His brother told Sam that in that respect he was lucky. Sam guesses Mark was right. Sam can't figure how he could ever pay the bills that have accumulated in the past four months. They're so astronomical they make him think of the budget deficit.

It's bad enough he has to make payments on the loan he took out to build their house. For two years Sam accepted as few outside jobs as possible, to concentrate on building a house for him and Amy. Sam loves the house he built. He installed hardwood floors and Andersen windows. The place may be small, but he didn't cut any corners when he put it up. And from the deck, he can still see green and blue without the interruption of high tension lines and satellite dishes.

Amy had smiled at the finished house last year, and at the kitchen Sam and two of his friends had customized for her, but sometimes she complained that the long drive to work at the Social Security Administration got to her. Once, after telling Sam in detail about her particularly frustrating day at work, she hadn't been in the mood to cook. She'd said, "You've got to drive twenty miles to get a goddamn slice of pizza out here."

Sign

Where Amy had grown up in Baltimore, take-out shops were as plentiful as the trees around their new property. Sam had held her and rubbed her back, then made them a couple of grilled cheese sandwiches.

Sam worries that if Amy wakes up she might say something he doesn't want to hear. Maybe she'll tell him it was a mistake for her to have left their apartment in Baltimore. Maybe she'll say he made things nice as he could for her, but she'd never been happy in the country, in the place where Sam grew up and has lived most of his life. But Sam worries even more that she won't wake up at all to confront him or to recognize his efforts to reach her, that maybe she's finally trying to leave him. Sam's brother tells him he's too hard on himself. Sam has stared at Amy's closed eyes for so many days, looking for the slightest indication that she can hear him, feel his presence, understand that he is crazy about her, that sometimes he forgets what day it is, even what month.

Sam has asked the doctors about her chances, but he can never get even a percentage from them. Weekends, he has gone to the library and read up on comas and traumas and tried to make some sense of what happened. The librarian even special-ordered some materials for him and then looked away, eyes lowered, after she handed them over. The most encouraging information Sam found not in the card catalog, but in a headline glaring from a newspaper rack in the A&P last week: "Singing Family Snaps Truck Driver Out of Ten-Month Coma." That gave him an idea. If "The Yellow Rose of Texas" sung by family members could rouse a man from ten months of oblivion, a significant song might be able to do the same for Amy, who's been lost to him less than half that time.

Sam has prepared a tape of three warm-up songs—favorites

he hopes will gently tempt her to return—and, finally, a fourth, the song that was played at their wedding, to thrust her back into the world. He pulls the tape player out of the bag, plugs it into an outlet farthest from the gurgling life-support machinery, and waits for the music to begin. If she has any doubts about her return, they will be wiped clean away when she hears "Imagine" playing and opens her eyes to him, sitting right beside her, holding her hand, with even more anxiety and love than he'd had the day, nearly seven years ago, when they were married. Sam had considered dressing in his wedding suit, but, in the end, decided that might be too hokey. Besides, he might look as if he were waiting for a funeral. For an hour, Sam rewinds and plays the tape at an increasingly loud volume. Finally, Joan peeks into the room.

"Sam, I'm afraid you're going to have to stop now. I'm getting complaints from some of the other patients."

"Sorry," he says. His hands are moist, his voice a little shaky; otherwise he would tell the nurse more. He'd explain how you have to go all out sometimes to get what you want.

"If it was just you, I'd let you bring a whole rock band in here, cutie," Joan says, sliding her hands into her uniform pockets, tightening the white material against her hips. Before closing the door she says, "Maybe they wouldn't mind so much if you were playing 'Moon River.' "

Next week he might have to bring a Walkman and two sets of headphones. He'd want to see Amy smiling and hear their wedding song at the same time. But nothing he's done has seemed to matter or to change her condition. Not the white chocolates he held under her nose then rubbed against her lips last month, not the explanations he's given her, the promises he's whispered. She hasn't changed since the day of the accident. He hasn't seen a flicker in her fingers or the slightest blink of an eye to let him know that he shouldn't give up hope that she's trying desperately to reach him. Amy looks so small, so innocent of everything they've done together that he wants to get on top of her, kiss her until she responds to him, calls his name. But there are so many bottles and tubes and dials. If something comes loose, he's been told, she couldn't make it on her own.

The evening of the accident, Sam and Amy had stopped by the Downeys' place. Joe had saddled up a gelding the color of worn blacktop, its mane and tail a broken line of white.

"He's quieter than a full-bellied pup," said Joe, giving the horse he'd bought just that morning a friendly slap across the rump.

Standing in front of the horse, Sam held onto the reins. He has determined, in all the times he's remembered this sequence of details, that he was the one to urge Amy onto the animal. Sam can't be sure, but he's fairly positive that the voice advising, "We'll make a country girl out of you yet, Amy," had been his own.

What happened next, Joe and Peg Downey and all his friends have assured him, could not have been avoided. Joe and Sam called out instructions to Amy—lean into him, pull to the right, tap with your left heel. Sometimes the men's words ran together, and they smiled at each other like boys who had collided during a field game. Without any warning, the animal took off suddenly, jumped the wooden corral fence Joe had put up the week before, and flung Amy into the air. It was as if the animal sensed Amy's ignorance of the terrain and chose that moment to display its power.

Strange as it might sound, Sam had almost laughed when

Amy went hurtling over the fence that resembled a goal post. She was always dancing and strutting around in funny ways to get him to laugh, but that was when they were alone. And when he'd reached her, all soft and sprawled, she looked almost the way she did when he left her early in the morning—her clothes like the covers in gentle folds around her small body. Sam had felt like a child spitting out the details of the accident to Peg, who'd been inside baking cornbread. His mind muddy, his whole body shook to wriggle itself free from the horrid tragedy.

Walking across the parking lot, Sam still smells the hospital near him, on him. The disinfectants and the gray color of day's end follow him right into the cab of his Toyota truck. He places the tape player on the passenger seat, slams the door, and fishes a cigarette from the breast pocket of his denim jacket. Smoke swirls around his face, and he flashes the golden high beams he installed after the first time a deer jumped in front of his truck.

As he drives northwest out of Baltimore, Sam knows it is going to happen again. Tonight. From out of nowhere a deer can bound in front of him and, just as quickly, disappear into the night fields. Or end up against his bumper. Sam estimates he's about thirty minutes away from the deer caution sign.

"Stupid animals," he says to comfort and ready himself. He runs his left hand through his hair.

The first time—two weeks ago—that Sam saw a deer after he'd left Amy's hospital bed, the animal jumped at his truck. Sam knows this is crazy, but the deer appeared to land from some place in the sky. The deer waited just long enough to freeze Sam in place, then took off. And last week, at the same spot in the road, there was another whir of motion. Sam saw the deer charging at him, but now he thinks the animal may have been running from him.

A few leaves skitter across the road, and instinctively Sam applies his brakes. With the streetlights of Baltimore far behind, it can be difficult to determine what's dead and what's alive.

The light from Marty's Food and Fuel, the last stopping place before home, soon crosses Sam's windshield.

"Hey, Marty," Sam yells as he's rolling down his window.

"Hey, guy," Marty calls, the way he does to everyone who stops. "Sam," he says when he gets closer, "you'd a thought I was givin' away hundred dollar bills the way you threw on them clinchers." Then Marty leans against Sam's truck and laughs until he wheezes.

Marty and Sam are about the same height, but Marty's got ten years on Sam and is at least twice as wide. Sam has always thought that Marty looks like he's been rubbed with sandpaper to give him that hairless, pink skin. When Sam once told Amy this, right here in front of Marty's, she laughed so enthusiastically her face reddened, and he could see the blush even along the part in her hair. Sam had reached over and kissed her on the mouth to calm her down.

"What can I do you for, Sam?"

"Smokes," says Sam, getting out of his truck. As he pays for the cigarettes, he asks Marty if he's seen any deer.

"Ain't huntin' season yet," Marty says without looking up from the change in his hands.

"No, I mean on the road."

"On the road." Marty scratches at his chin. "Not lately." He pauses, "You've got to watch them. They can do a number on your vehicle. I don't care if you're drivin' a damn tank."

When Sam drives off, he thinks not of the drivers and their cars, but of the deer that have died. How with all the new houses going up, the animals have been displaced and forced to flee to confusing new surroundings. On either side of this road, hundreds of house lights sparkle in the dark. The farms and forests he knew when he and Amy were first married are now an infestation of small ranch houses, the boundaries of each one perforated by a chain-link fence. With the number of new construction sites Sam pours concrete for every month, he can't imagine where all of the animals will go. Sam lights another cigarette.

"Five miles," Sam says aloud. A roadside shack is Sam's way of noting the distance to where the incidents with the deer have happened. And just a half mile beyond will appear the sign, after the fact—an image of a dark animal form jumping against a background the color of morning sunshine.

Sam is considering that not only will a deer meet him tonight at this place, but also that this deer is the same deer he's seen twice before. He is giving the deer more significance than he could ever have imagined, driving farther and farther from his motionless wife, who no longer has anything to do with songs she loved or with all the people whose names he's whispered to her. Or with him.

As the defroster growls, Sam thinks there's nothing really to protect him from what will happen. Not headlights or slower speeds, or hospitals, or wives. Or silence.

Maybe three is the number of times it takes most people to learn things. Or at least to recognize them.

The steering wheel has become slippery with sweat. Sam imagines that somehow his wife can see him driving toward disaster, maybe even directing him. He feels moisture in the corners of his eyes begin to blur his vision. He will show her, which is more than she has done for him, her eyes, dull bottomless circles beneath translucent lids.

Sign

In four months Amy has shown him nothing at all. He wants an indication that things will change. He prays for it. If he hits the deer and it dies, if he hits the deer and he dies, that will be clear and understandable.

"Amy," he yells.

He doesn't slow his truck but drives through the spot where it happened before. Nothing.

Nothing.

His hands and face are wet. And what he feels is not relief, but disappointment. All day as he mixed the light sand and cement, and poured and leveled the gray concrete, then as he drove toward the hospital, he had hoped for Amy to respond to the music, to him. And when that didn't work, he anticipated spotting the deer again, hitting it at full force—finally assuming the impact of all he's done, or should do.

The tilted cautionary square, the color of golden light with a black animal's form extended in flight, comes into Sam's view, then into focus. Just behind this marker, on the edge of the dark road, he spots a deer frozen in the light. The animal is as still as a lawn ornament. He drives by, watching its eyes glow like two tiny stop signs, until the darkness takes over again.

Working Women

Martha read the note on the refrigerator: "Martha—DO NOT EAT. Eugene's taking us out tonight. Love, Mom." Most nights for the last couple of months, Linda's message to Martha had identified what was for dinner and how it should be heated up: frequently, "covered, 350 degrees, 45 minutes." Before Martha started working for the *Herald,* she and Linda had prepared the meal and eaten together every afternoon. Afterward Linda went off to the University Hospital, where she worked the evening shift as a nurse's aide. Martha was usually still up studying when her mother arrived back home after midnight with a good half hour's worth of stories, mostly from the emergency room, and the two would have a snack and talk in front of some late-night movie. But after Martha finished college and got the newspaper job, the routine altered. Linda left for work at three-thirty; Martha got home after six. Martha guessed that things would have changed anyway, with Eugene coming into the picture and all.

Linda hadn't had many boyfriends since her divorce from Martha's father—not that Martha had seen. The first winter they were alone, Jimmy Silver had banged on their front door at eight o'clock one Sunday morning until Linda had cracked the door and hissed, "I've got a daughter asleep in here for

God's sake. Now go on home." And Martha didn't remember even stopping as she was quickly introduced to a prickly-faced man called Draw Evers when she and her mother were on their way to the Italian festival a couple of summers ago. When Martha had asked, "Why's his name Draw?" her mother hadn't answered but had said simply, "Never mind about him." Usually Martha didn't hear Linda talk about men as anything other than patients or doctors, as if both of those classifications rendered them sexless. The ones who did make overt passes, Linda described in detail to Martha and then dismissed with the line, "Same symptoms, different disease." The phrase always made Martha laugh.

Martha hadn't met Eugene yet, but she'd heard his voice on the phone a couple of times. He had more of a southern accent than the usual Baltimore one, and he always sounded as if he were about to reveal important information. "That Eugene is such a card," Linda said. Martha opened the refrigerator and, more out of defiance than hunger, cut herself a large wedge of Swiss cheese.

An hour later, Linda arrived at the house with Eugene. Though Eugene was heavy and in places his white scalp showed through the fair hair combed straight back from his forehead, Martha could see that he was younger than her mother. Not so young that someone might mistake him for Linda's son, and probably closer to Linda's age than to Martha's, but younger nonetheless. Even though she could just squeeze into a size 14, Linda was about half Eugene's size. Tonight she wore strings of glass beads at her neck and wrists along with a couple of metallic bracelets, and a bright shade of lipstick. She'd recently taken to "touching up" her reddish hair.

"Eugene, this is my sweet gal I've told you all about," she

said. Her voice was higher than normal and Martha could smell her minty breath. Linda stared proudly at her daughter while Eugene hesitated, as if wondering whether to shake Martha's hand or to embrace her. Martha smiled perfunctorily and took a step backward in the direction of her bedroom. Without allowing the smile to leave her face, she excused herself to get ready for the outing.

"Where you keep the cold ones around here?" Martha heard Eugene say. She listened to his heavy footsteps as he circled the kitchen and stopped in front of the refrigerator. Since her father had moved out ten years earlier, the little Baltimore row house had forgotten the noticeable sounds of men. The dark bottles clinked against one another when Eugene swung the refrigerator door open. Martha listened to her mother's jewelry tinkling in the kitchen, the living room, the bathroom, and the thuds of Eugene's feet following, muffled in carpet.

Eugene drove Martha and Linda to the White Cat in Fells Point in his new Dodge Dart. The horn honked whenever any part of the steering wheel was squeezed, and Eugene hadn't gotten used to it yet. "Sure is sensitive," he said when an elderly woman on the sidewalk glared at him. Linda laughed softly.

Before dinner, the three walked down to the waterfront to watch the ships and the sun setting behind them. Linda and Eugene argued playfully over whether one of the ships was Italian or Spanish. Because Martha didn't want to interfere and tell Eugene *he* was right, she absently watched the movements in the harbor. Ships and sailboats appeared to almost collide as a light breeze seemed to push them together.

Linda was in a silly mood, the way she got sometimes when she was comfortably sunk into the living room sofa after a twelve-hour shift at the hospital. Those times Martha would get her mother a beer and, by the time it was gone, mother and daughter would be giggling together. Today Linda spoke to Eugene, instead. "Doesn't the sky look all gooey, Eugene? I never have seen the sun looking that way." When nobody responded, she said, "I read it's because of all the chemicals they pump into the air these days."

"Well, I guess we'll just have to wait and see what the moon looks like," Eugene said flatly, his arms folded against his large chest.

Linda laughed and laughed above Eugene's voice. Martha quickly saw the difference between her father and Eugene. Her father had tried to be funny but usually wasn't. Eugene didn't even try, and yet he entertained Linda. Eugene prepared Linda for a laugh by saying things like, "You'll like this one, Linda," or "Wait till you get a load of this." Martha was sure that Eugene told stories raw—exactly as they'd happened or been told to him—and didn't embellish them as her father had done.

When Martha's father had lived with them, he'd worked as a cook at a number of different Baltimore diners and chain restaurants. A couple of years ago, Linda heard he had become a chef in a fancy restaurant in Philadelphia.

In the beginning, right after the divorce, Martha spent weekends with her father at his apartment. Saturday mornings he'd stop by for her and they'd go shopping together. He'd say, "What kind of spaghetti does your mother use?" In response, Martha always selected new brands she'd unsuccessfully tried to get her mother to buy. When her father finally stopped picking her up on weekends, she was certain that somehow he'd found out she'd deceived him: it was Nestlé's Linda used, not Ovaltine; Chicken of the Sea, not Bumblebee.

Martha knew that if she and Eugene ever went shopping together he'd select the brands he wanted, not because he didn't care to hear Martha's opinion, but because he'd want to convince Martha and Linda of his own choices. Each selection would be one more item in the long list of specifics that comprised his character. Eugene wouldn't buy the most expensive meats or exotic imported bottles of delicacies, but would stand firmly behind his favorite brand of catsup. Martha had to admire that kind of confidence.

Eugene was also noticeably larger than Martha's father. In addition to being overweight, Eugene was strong. He stood about six inches taller than Linda as he put his arms around them and said, "A table for three, please," in the foyer of the White Cat. Even though his grip on her shoulder would possibly leave marks, five tiny impressions that would turn pale green and then yellow before entirely melting away, Martha could tell that the inclusive semicircle Eugene made of his arms impressed Linda.

Martha put a mental frame around the picture of the three of them: Linda, chubby and happy in her new purple dress; Martha more slender than her mother, tall like her father, and much fairer than either of them; Eugene between the women, a cigarette tucked behind his ear, and wearing a pale blue shirt. The shirt, which he explained he'd sent away for, featured a tiny TV set in place of the usual alligator. Eugene repaired television sets for a living. He smoothed his shirt with the palms of his hands and passed a couple of folded-over bills to the hostess who directed them to a table.

Once seated, Eugene demonstrated to Linda that he was a family-oriented man. He ordered "wine for the ladies," and, after a beat, changed his own request from beer to wine. Not until Linda left the table to buy cigarettes did Eugene calm down. For the first few moments that Linda was gone, he and Martha didn't know what to say.

"Your mother and I have a lot of fun together," he said finally, seriously. Martha sipped her wine then looked up at him as if he'd just apologized for something. "It's not what you're thinking," he said. Martha studied a painted wooden cutout of a huge white cat holding a smiling fish between its paws.

"Your mother's something else." Then he added, "I'm sure I'm not telling you anything." His lowered eyes, the way he gently rolled and unrolled the edge of the damp cocktail napkin, made Martha imagine that this man saw a bit of what she saw in Linda—the warm smile and eyes, the open arms that accepted the merest hint of accomplishment as success itself. But Martha's identification with Eugene lasted only until Linda came into view.

Linda was smoking on her way back to the table. The stream from her cigarette and the large puff from her mouth flowed behind her like a long, ghostly scarf. Eugene pulled out Linda's chair and patted it as if he'd trained her for something, and the two of them were about to perform.

"How's the newspaper business?" Eugene asked Martha. He winked at Linda. He had conveniently waited to inquire about her job until Linda was present to hear the concern in his voice.

"I guess Linda's told you," said Martha. Linda told everyone she knew that her only daughter worked for the area's major newspaper.

"It's pretty busy this time of year," said Martha, trying to make her voice sound as matter-of-fact as Eugene's. "I write up the weddings," she added, knowing she didn't have to explain her ambition to be a reporter. Eugene's hand snaked into Martha's view and settled on Linda's forearm. Without looking up, Martha could tell that Eugene and her mother were grinning at each other.

The number of wedding and engagement announcements mailed to the society section of the *Sunday Herald* hadn't leveled off since Martha began working there. Every day, Martha drank a cup of light coffee as she opened the envelopes containing photos and the written details of each event. "There's always a backlog," Catherine, Martha's coworker, told her. "People never seem to stop getting married." Catherine spoke the word "married" as if it were as routine as watching television.

Catherine was thin, with short, light brown hair curling toward the edges of a mouth that seldom smiled. Her skin was so white and stretched so tightly over her small frame that, to Martha, she looked translucent. If Catherine weren't so impeccably groomed and well dressed, she would have appeared to be recuperating from a terrible disease. Martha was friendly to Catherine, who sat directly across from her, but she didn't trust her.

"Good morning, girls," the section editor, Betsy Dashfellow, said in a cultivated accent, oddly combining English gentility and southern twang. Betsy never looked at the person to whom she directed a comment. Betsy was tall and thin, and everything about her, including her makeup and her jet-black hair, was dangerously close to overdone. Yet she maintained a sense of decorum, because she knew precisely how much polite society would tolerate.

Betsy was fifty-six and had never been married. Martha knew there was a story behind that, which she hoped Catherine would reveal. But Catherine wasn't the type to tell a story for mere enjoyment; she took herself too seriously. Besides, Catherine was grooming herself for Betsy's job, unlike Martha, who was just gathering résumé time until she was offered a reporting job.

After Betsy finished reading *Women's Wear Daily* and the *New York Times,* Catherine handed her the opened stack of photos and announcements, which had arrived in the morning mail. Betsy followed a routine that, Martha guessed, had been established many years earlier. Flipping through photos attached to typed or handwritten pages, Betsy selected the socially prominent brides and the recently engaged who would decorate page one of her social section. Those young women were entitled to the page with the fewest and consequently the largest photographs, the most lengthy articles, headlines like "Miss Larson Weds Mr. Peterson in Roland Park," and the company of their own kind. If, in her initial scan through the announcements, Betsy did not recognize a name as an influential family in Baltimore, she consulted her *Social Register.* Sometimes a prestigious photographer—Odel or Bachrach—made Betsy stop and consider the pictured woman as one who might be entitled to appear on page one in spite of being an unknown. In addition, Betsy had a list of socially acceptable zip codes, as well as a map with the best sections of the city highlighted in a pale, ice blue.

And she made comments: "God, look at this one" or "Can you believe anyone actually thinking this dress is appropriate for a wedding?" By the time Betsy finished critiquing, she had three piles of announcements in front of her—preliminary placement, she called it. One stack, the smallest, would go on her select page. Another pile of young women from professional and successful, if not socially recognized, families was directed to Martha for page two. The remainder of the announcements, termed "page three placement," in actuality might fit above or alongside ads for lingerie and flatware and store openings and closings, on any one of the section's eight back pages. Catherine handled the page three announcements which, by the time they were published, would feature faces reduced to the size of quarters.

Each woman took her appropriate pile of photos and began telephoning to verify Betsy Dashfellow's initial instinct about social position.

"Good morning, Mrs. Watson," Martha said, then introduced herself politely to the person on the other end of the phone. Pleasantly, she went through the details of the wedding—spelling names and addresses, reading back the particulars of the couple's schooling—and listened to Mrs. Watson's comments on the cake and the photographer. The more specifics she endured, the easier the final question would be to ask. Finally Martha asked it, "What does the bride's father do for a living?" While the families of page three brides may have indecipherable ethnic names, they were proud to say they were plumbers or steam fitters or deli managers. Martha's page two families usually turned the question right back to her. Mrs. Watson cleared her throat and said, "Are you going to be printing this personal information in the newspaper, dear? I really don't see how it's relevant." That was the uncomfortable moment of every call, when Martha truly hated her boss, despised the whole notion of placement and society. She couldn't wait until she'd put in her time and could move on to the newsroom.

The employment information obtained from "verifying" an announcement could change everything. Martha traded Catherine a carpenter for a franchise owner; Catherine handed Martha an Eastern Shore farmer who made over forty thousand dollars a year, and, in return, Martha gave Catherine a bride whose father was deceased and whose mother was a hairdresser in East Baltimore.

"She's cute," Martha stopped to say about Miss Tabolowsker before handing a photo to Catherine, hoping to bring some value to the young woman whose wedding account was being relegated to the underwear ads and underclasses.

"Don't patronize her," Catherine said, surprising Martha.

Occasionally one of Martha's brides—perhaps the offspring of two lawyers—moved to Betsy's page one. Certain things, however, never changed after verification, no matter how much money was involved: a Jew seldom moved to page one, a black woman to page two.

Martha wished she could confide to Catherine that she didn't think marriage made much sense. Let alone shuffling around peoples' lives like playing cards. Let alone the situation of her mother and Eugene Petts.

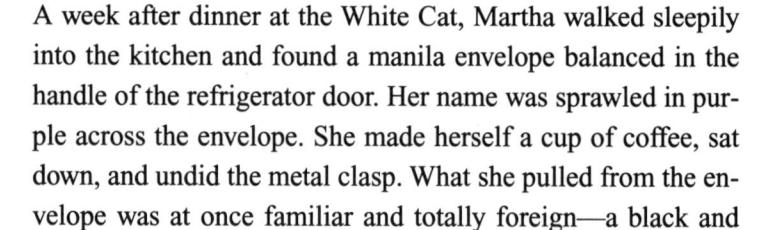

A week after dinner at the White Cat, Martha walked sleepily into the kitchen and found a manila envelope balanced in the handle of the refrigerator door. Her name was sprawled in purple across the envelope. She made herself a cup of coffee, sat down, and undid the metal clasp. What she pulled from the envelope was at once familiar and totally foreign—a black and white glossy photograph of her mother.

In the five-by-seven portrait, Linda's skin was smooth, her eyes soft and dark, her bits of gray hair that poked through the "touching up" unnoticeable. The tiny hoop earrings she always wore, no matter what other jewelry was around her wrists or neck, sparkled.

Looking at the photograph, Martha could see where she'd gotten her own looks, not beautiful but attractive. Linda was wearing the V-neck pullover that Martha had given her for her birthday.

Paperclipped to the photo was a carefully-printed paragraph beginning with "Nurse's Aide to Wed Eugene Petts." Not until Martha neared the end of the announcement—the line that revealed Eugene's place of employment as Tony's TV—did she clearly understand that she was reading not some paragraph that was part of her job, but news of her mother.

Linda had copied exactly the format of the engagement notices that Martha wrote every working day. The final line read, "A November wedding is planned." Martha had hoped that the closing would be the line that always revealed a more uncertain couple, "A wedding date has not been set."

Returning the photo to its envelope, Martha noticed a note in her mother's large-lettered style, "Do what you can, honey. Love, Mom." Martha immediately translated "do what you can" to "try to get me on a page with a decent-size photo. Page two. Your page." Practically everyone whom Martha spoke to during verification asked about the large photos and long write-ups—how could they get the prominence they so deserved? Many offered to pay Martha for a position of distinction. Martha promised them nothing but said, "I'll do what I can."

Catherine and Martha sat across from each other in the newspaper cafeteria. As usual, Martha had brought a couple of magazines to read during the long lapses in conversation. Face down on top of the two magazines was a photograph that Chick Forney from the art department had passed to Martha earlier: an eight-by-ten glossy of a bride on which Chick had worked his airbrushing magic.

Martha said, "Will you look at this?" mocking Betsy's drawl. She held up the photo featuring exposed breasts and a cigarette dangling from the bride's lips. Martha hoped to erase job delineations and coax Catherine to her with a laugh, as she once had done with her mother. Suddenly, Martha missed the afternoons when she and Linda exchanged stories and prepared casseroles.

She smiled at Catherine's horrified expression and assured her that the photo was not an original but a tampered-with duplicate.

"It's just a joke," Martha said, relieved at the hint of a smile in Catherine's face. Without saying anything, Catherine went on peeling her huge orange.

"Can you ever imagine submitting your wedding announcement to Betsy?" Martha asked.

Catherine looked up but continued to work on the orange. "Why, yes," she said.

Martha wondered how she could ask Betsy to consider her mother's picture, hidden in her briefcase. She knew that she couldn't tell Linda that Betsy didn't approve of engagement announcements the second time around. Betsy didn't need to know the relationship between Martha and the woman in the photo; Linda had taken back her maiden name right after her divorce.

"I mean she'd be studying it the way she does. Looking for the slightest detail to make you feel inadequate."

"We automatically get page two," Catherine said, reminding Martha of one of the "benefits" of working for the paper.

Martha wanted to ask Catherine—hypothetically—if the benefit extended to family members. Instead, Martha said, "I know, but I wouldn't want her handling my photograph."

Catherine shook her head at the remark and began to separate the sections of the orange.

Martha studied her coworker—her delicate, ordinary features and fine hair. Catherine, she imagined, lived in a house with unblemished white walls, polished hardwood floors, a pool and patio, and had spent years in classrooms of uniformed girls, brushed smooth of uniqueness. The scent of Catherine's orange seemed to latch onto Martha's clothing and stick there.

Martha could probably get her mother's picture on page two by affixing a phony verification date in the upper right-hand corner, and penciling in the word "manager" near Eugene's job. But certain facts that normally applied only to page three brides couldn't be ignored: the addresses of Linda and Eugene were not within the icy blue borders of Betsy's map.

After lunch Martha began entering headlines into the computer: "Miss Feirstein to Wed Dr. Small;" "Miss Tarangtella, Economist, Weds Mr. Rasmussen;" "Miss Gordon, of Randallstown, Engaged." When the announcements were in this form—light green words on a sea of darker green, without the distraction of yearning eyes or pleading voices—it was easy to see who belonged where. Martha had made the correct choices.

Deciding on her mother's social place in the paper, Martha felt as coldly objective as Betsy Dashfellow. Her mother did not belong on page two, but among the hairstylists and saleswomen and wives of plumbers and tool and dye makers.

Linda's situation was clear-cut. Martha felt her own life, if placed on the social page, would be the difficult case, the bright East Baltimore girl with professional ambitions that defied the expectations of her neighborhood. The daughter of a possibly well-known chef, future step-daughter of a TV repairman, she would never be at home in either Betsy's page two or page three classifications. She would prefer to float unseen somewhere between the two.

Bags and papers crinkling in his arms, Eugene knocked on the front door. Linda was wearing her pink terry-cloth robe when she kissed him good morning and started coffee. She hadn't yet combed out her hair, and her voice was husky with sleep. Dressed in a plaid sports coat, Eugene had stopped by for breakfast after church. He pulled rolls and jelly doughnuts from the brown bags and arranged them on a plate he located after trying only two cupboard doors.

The three of them sat down, the *Sunday Herald* in the middle of the kitchen table. Winking at her daughter, Linda grabbed the society section first, as she'd done every Sunday since Martha began working at the paper.

"Damn Birds," Eugene said at the headlines in the sports section. Slurping at his coffee, he looked at ease. How quickly he had settled into Linda's life. Eugene would never whisk Linda off to Hawaii for the weekend, but he would make popcorn for her before her favorite sitcom. He wore his confidence better than he wore clothing, Martha thought. Betsy Dashfellow's self-assurance, on the other hand, seemed applied. Not like ordinary makeup, but like stage makeup.

Martha drank orange juice and watched her mother light a cigarette and then slowly page through the faces of the brides and engaged women as if it were an album of family photos.

"Oh, honey," Linda said suddenly. She turned the page for her and Eugene to see.

"It's wonderful." As Linda read the announcement aloud, Martha thought she could see her mother's eyes beginning to water and her tears hanging there instead of spilling over onto the network of lines on her skin as delicate as pencil marks. Eugene, maybe sensing this, put his arm around Linda and together they stared at the announcement in silence.

Linda's face, the size of a child's watch, looked out from the section's seventh page. The features blurred in black newsprint. To her left was a prominent ad for a new perfume that a soap opera star would be promoting on Wednesday. To the right, the features of a woman majoring in cosmetology faced in the same direction as Linda's. Both pairs of eyes seemed to be looking at an ad on the far side of the page for free ear piercing at Sally's Salon.

Eugene was smiling proudly, even as he looked up at Martha and said, almost under his breath, "I thought you had some pull." But Linda merely patted his hand and smiled over the picture.

Linda folded the page back, then into quarters where her face was centered among lines of type. Her mouth trembled when she looked at Martha. "Oh, darling," she said. "This is lovely. This is so wonderful."

Eugene cleared his throat and stood up to refill the coffee cups.

"You'll never know how happy I am," Linda said, now crying openly. As Martha repeated the words silently, she felt her own eyes filling with tears.

"Same symptoms, different disease," she whispered, but Linda didn't hear her.

Sauna

*W*es starts the fire for sauna. A few yards away, Liza plants potatoes—turning the best eyes upward, then sprinkling dirt into the holes.

Outside the sauna building, double the size of an outhouse, Wes splits scrap wood for the fire. He disappears again, and the iron door of the wood stove creaks open and closed as he feeds the flames. By the time Liza has buried the last piece of potato, smoke rushes from the sauna's chimney, then onto the buds and sprays of green in the tallest oaks. Before smoke can mix with sky, a wind catches and drives some of it down and over the creek. For a few moments smoke idles over the water, fast from recent thaws.

Early in their marriage Wes and Liza did this twice a week: started and stoked the fire to 200 degrees, peeled off their clothing, sat on the wooden benches in the small dark room until sweat seeped, then flowed like some inner spring, from their bodies. When they couldn't stand the heat any longer, they ran from it and leapt into the chilly creek. Even on the coldest days, when ice sealed the creek like a lid, they went through the ritual. Wes walked carefully out onto the ice and cut a hole large enough to lower themselves through. Afterward, they were exhilarated and exhausted.

These days they take a steam once, maybe twice, a month, and never in the cold months. Today's is the first sauna Wes has made this year.

Although, over the years, their habits have changed and the time between certain routines has lengthened, Wes still promotes sauna as a cure-all for everything from an aching back to a sunburn. The body opens to the intense heat, and dirt and tension evacuate like people running from a burning house. Then cold water closes the pores so that no impurities can reenter. Those moments when nothing's allowed back in astonish Liza with the pleasure she finds in her own body.

"Genetics," Wes said recently when Liza wondered for the first time if the temperature extremes might hurt his heart. "I come from hearty stock." His grandfather Eetu, in his nineties, drank a quart of vodka and took sauna every day. Eetu beat himself regularly with a stick to heighten circulation and to hurry the deepest-hidden dirt from his body.

"American diet," Liza replied, to strengthen her position in what never developed into a full-fledged argument.

Years ago, when they were getting used to living together, Wes and Liza took saunas after they had a fight. Those weren't the only times they steamed themselves into submission, but Liza remembers with relief how the anger was liquified and drawn out of their bodies. When the misunderstanding disappeared with the burnt logs, Liza was glad to be alone, once again, with Wes.

"How about a beer?" Wes calls as he walks up the dirt path to the house his father built. Wes's father was born in Finland and arrived in New York at nineteen. Though he found a wife and a construction job quickly enough, Kari wasn't satisfied. He couldn't imagine taking sauna on the banks of the East

River. Wes was a toddler by the time his father had saved up enough money to move the family north in search of a place to build a house and a Finnish steam room. He stopped three hours north of the city. Then there were only trees, no neighbors or even a store within fifteen miles. Five hundred yards from the spot where Kari built his house, the creek still bends through firs and saplings into perfect seclusion.

"Keep an eye on that fire," Wes hollers. Wes built this sauna, the second one, fifteen years ago, after the original burned down. Leaves on the roof of that one were hit by a chimney spark. The roof caught fire and nearly took the surrounding woods with it.

Liza picks up a few dead branches and breaks them to stove size, then adds them to the fire along with some pieces of wood that were once a neighbor's fence. The fire pops, and not so far off, the grind and growl of machinery sounds again. The high-pitched beep means some more trees are coming down, a new house going up.

Wes learned carpentry from his father. Sometimes he subcontracts to do finishing work on the houses growing up around them. Mostly they will become the homes of IBM employees. The money is good, and Wes enjoys making cabinets and door frames, but he's told Liza that he doesn't like to think of the trees thinning like hair before his eyes.

Besides towels and beer, Wes has a radio. The music used to irritate Liza, who prefers the sound of the water moving over and around rocks, wind in dry leaves, birdsong, or simply silence. Now the songs distract her from the nearby noises of construction.

Wes pops two Buds and hands one to Liza. "So. Are we all set for Saturday?" Saturday's the party, Wes and Liza's twenty-fifth anniversary. Liza has rented a band and a tent, and hired a caterer.

"I think everything's under control," she says.

Actually, the only thing not settled about the party is Liza. If it were her decision, if it weren't so late, she'd call the whole thing off. But now that she's gotten Wes excited about the celebration, there's no backing out. "I haven't tapped a keg of beer in years," was the first thing he'd said when she brought up the idea.

When Liza had first asked Wes about the party, she thought the only guests should be those who were witnesses to their years together. For months, Wes and Liza talked about what they'd eat and who they'd invite. Finally, to avoid hurt feelings, they invited just about everyone they knew. Liza made a list of names that stretched from Aunt Charlene to Bud and Jane Tidy, a couple she and Wes had met recently at the bowling alley.

Liza sealed and mailed 100 invitations, and now she wonders about their decision. Most of these people have no idea that she and Wes are still happy, that this landmark anniversary is a celebration of romance that has survived.

Wes checks the sauna's temperature on the thermometer mounted on the wall and adds wood to the fire. "The water's mighty cold." He winks and teases, "Do you have the heart for this?" Liza knows it pleases him that, like the bravest of Finns, she always runs right from the steam room into the cold water.

"My grandfather would have been proud of the woman I married," Wes once said to her. "You're no Finn, but you could almost pass." He touched her black hair and laughed. His hair had been fine and blonde then and, when it was wet and clinging to his head, indistinguishable from his scalp.

Liza had met him in town, in the family candy store that's hers now. A few days before Easter, the store had been packed; before the mall was built, everybody bought their holiday candy from Liza's father. She spotted Wes moving slowly through the small room as he examined the chocolate bunnies and eggs and hats she'd helped her father make and wrap with cellophane. Between ringing up orders, she noticed his long arms. When he reached the cash register with nothing in his hands, she looked at him straight on. "Could I help you with something?" On the other side of the glass he pointed at the assorted dark chocolates. Months later, he told her he loved it that she didn't blink and lower her eyes like other girls.

He came back the next day for another pound. Two weeks after Easter, they were married in a small ceremony at St. Stanislaus Church.

Wes said an engagement and a big party weren't important, and Liza didn't disagree. Maybe she got the idea to have the twenty-fifth anniversary party because they had missed out on a wedding celebration. But now she wishes Saturday could be more like their wedding day—dining with a small group of friends after the ceremony—instead of 100 acquaintances scattered over the yard like seeds.

It's a wonder Wes wants the party. Whenever they're at a gathering of more than a dozen people, she finds him off reading a book, looking at photographs, or talking to the host's dog. Around other people, he doesn't say more than has to be said.

"Wes, do you still want to go through with this?"

"Come on, it's not that cold."

"The party. You still want to have it?"

Wes finishes his beer. "Liza, it's the day after tomorrow. We've got everything paid for and ready to go." Wes always completes what he's started; she remembers the time he finished a set of bookshelves for a customer who refused to pay. "I have to complete the job," he said to her when she called him a fool.

Trucks and levelers nearby groan over the song on the radio. Some of the people they've invited live in the white or beige or slate blue ranch houses planted in rows along the road.

"One seventy," Wes calls as he checks the thermometer again. He opens another beer. After Liza rinses her hands in the creek, she sets out what she'll need for later—moisturizer, clean underwear, a comb.

On Saturday, some of the guests will wander down here. Liza pictures Wes, an eager host, proudly pointing out where he caught the six-pound trout, where the turtles lay their rubbery eggs, and where the giant eel slipped through his handmade netting. He might entertain his visitors by explaining how sauna is taken in the old country. Someone is sure to giggle, someone else to object to the shock to the body. And Wes will point to himself and to Liza as evidence that the process is a good one, a healthy one.

"We should cook up the sauna on Saturday," he says. His blonde hair is silver but still soft as a boy's.

"We'll kill off half the party."

"I'm serious."

"So am I. Wes, most people aren't used to this kind of thing. Most of these people have never even taken a cold shower."

Wes kisses her lightly on the lips. "Come on," he says.

In the dressing area where they usually take opposite chairs, she folding her pants and shirt and socks as soon as she removes them, his clothes dropping into a heap by his feet, Wes approaches her. Staring at her face, he touches her blouse. His callused fingers seem too large to press the small white buttons through their appropriate holes. Before she can protest this violation of their ritual, he has undone the blouse, peeled the cloth back from her breasts, and pulled it past her shoulders. Then, gently, he holds her off from him the way he does with the newspaper when he doesn't have his reading glasses.

She is a little embarrassed at this study because her body, though still thin, has loosened in places and become mottled with freckles. She's read that these tiny signs of accumulated abuse from the sun appear years after exposure.

His body is still fair and strong. She had thought Wes would always look the same as when they were married at twenty-four, until one morning eight years ago when he was shaving and she was brushing her teeth. Suddenly, with an unexpected flash of objectivity, Liza saw clearly the lines at their foreheads and eyes.

"Wes," she pleads now. "This party. I think it's a mistake."

No one who will be at the party on Saturday, no one anywhere for that matter, knows how she and Wes fit together in sleep or how they talk to each other when they're dreaming. They've woken a couple of times in the middle of a conversation.

There was a time once, for a few weeks, when Liza thought they might not make it. She can't say there was a specific problem. It was when both their parents were alive; before they had a house or a candy store; when one of them believed, for a time, what they'd been told—a child is proof of your love.

He kisses her and says softly, "How could it be a mistake? It will be fun. We'll see people we haven't seen in years."

As he slides the blouse off her arms, he says, "After everyone leaves, we'll come back here. Just the two of us. We'll leave the lights out. Like it used to be. Before we had electric down here." He puts his hand in her hair the way he does when she reads to him. Despite her worries about the party, she feels herself relax. Sometimes she thinks he can read the lines across her forehead better than a fortune teller keys into the heart lines of a palm.

What Wes cannot detect in her face is something she hasn't yet told him. She's only just discovered it herself. The decision they put off, the thing that would have made them more like the people coming to their party, has finally been determined. She can no longer have a child. She wonders if by fall she will shrink and dry to the color of rust like the leaves on their white oaks, then float off from the sturdy foundation of herself.

They used to joke that if she were pregnant, she couldn't take sauna for nine months or more. But the real reason she and Wes remained childless was to ensure that they would continue to be complete in themselves. Liza thinks she and Wes still get along so well because they have ceremony in their lives—an omelet every Monday morning, bowling on Friday evenings. It was Wes who said kids kick the hell out of rituals.

Putting his arms around her, Wes undoes Liza's beige-colored bra, covers her small breasts with his hands, then pulls her against his chest covered with a mist of gray hair. She touches the back of his neck, his shoulders, works her way down along his arms.

"Remember?" he says.

She nods into his chest. He means the time shortly after they met when they made love on the top bench in the steam room. But that had been before they'd stoked the fire to nearly 200 degrees.

Wes helps Liza with her pants, then he works his own off as

well. On the side of Wes's calf, a prominent blue vein wriggles an indirect path toward his foot. She thinks her legs must be the color of raw chicken, but at least they've held to the hard curve of muscle.

Last night in bed, she reached for Wes. In all their years of marriage, she can count on two hands the times she's initiated lovemaking. Not that she doesn't want Wes as much as he wants her. It's just that over time they've become so attuned to each other's needs that he simply, dutifully, forges ahead the way he does everything. Wes is the first one out of bed every morning, even when she has to leave for work before him.

Yet, last night, instead of rolling over to face him, turning into his kiss, Liza got onto her knees beside him. She kissed his neck and chest and stomach. She knelt on top of him, then dropped a leg to either side of his waist, bent forward to meet another kiss. He kneaded her back and breasts. Pulling off from him, she looked at his face lit by a pale shade of moonlight. His eyes were closed when she lowered herself onto him.

As he held her by the waist, she moved against him. He reached for her shoulders, to turn her, but she fought to stay on top.

Liza now sits on Wes's lap as he slides her knee-high socks from her legs. He strokes her legs so attentively and lightly that she is certain he's forgetting completely about time and how it's changed both of them.

"It's time to go in," he says.

Liza laughs as she takes off the barrette holding her gray-streaked hair in a bun at the back of her head. Outside, the birds dip in and out among the branches tipped with green. The forsythia shows off a bit of gold. Liza removes her wedding ring.

Carrying a bucket full of cold creek water, Wes goes in first, and Liza closes the steam door behind them. He pours a dipper of water on the place where she usually sits, to cool it. "There you go," he says and then proceeds to cool down his own spot beside hers. The old sauna was a truly dark room, but this one has a small window. She likes to watch what's going on outside. Sometimes smoke blows past.

"Wes," she starts to say, to tell him about her body. His "Shhh" is quickly hidden by the hiss of water hitting hot rocks.

The night they married, Liza thought one or both of them would die. She lay awake not believing that anything could be so perfect, that maybe she wasn't deserving of such happiness. She remembered her aunt's magazines that reported strange, remote happenings—an engaged couple each driving to see the other and colliding midway; lovers in South America found petrified by lava, yet still holding hands.

Wes tosses more water on the dark stones. They spit back, and steam squeezes Liza like a great, hot hand.

"Ouch," she hollers. Wes dribbles cold water on her head to cool her down. When he throws more water on the rocks, she starts to sweat. Sweat is running down Wes's chest and onto the bench below, where he rests his feet. His hand goes up to his brow.

"What we have to do is keep the men from going off to play cards and the women from sitting together and exchanging new ways to use sun-dried tomatoes," Liza reminds him. "And from showing photos of their kids," she adds.

"That's why we got the band. Remember?" he says and smiles. "Don't worry about the party. It'll be fine. You'll see." After a moment he says, "This is great." He's absolutely right, Liza thinks.

Wes gives her a washcloth he's dipped in the water bucket and she presses it into her hot face. "Ready for another blast?" he wants to know.

"A little one. Just a little." He throws a bit of water on the rocks. As the steam sneaks up around her, she imagines it pulling the dirt out from under her fingernails, dissolving the freckles splattered over her body.

"How much longer will we be able to do this?" Liza asks him. He stares at her. "Take sauna," she clarifies.

"There's no reason why we can't when we're ninety."

She cuts him off before he gets started on Eetu. "No. I mean before all the trees are cut down and this place isn't private anymore. Before people can watch us from their picture windows."

Wes is sweating so much he looks like he's melting. "We've still got a half acre on the other side of the creek." Then he reaches for her shoulder and easily slides his hand down her arm. "Who's gonna look at our old bodies anyway?" He laughs and holds her. If he squeezes, she thinks, she's slippery enough to pop out of his arms. "Forget it," he says. And she does. She lets worry drain from her arms and legs and face and chest.

The secret Liza has learned after years of taking sauna is this: stay in one minute beyond what you can bear. It makes coming out all the better.

Soon after she met him, Wes brought her here when his parents were away. It was March and the sky was foggy with snow. When they'd sweated all she could stand and run onto the creek, their feet stuck to the ice. Because the hole that Wes had sawed open for them had healed back, he pulled her down on the bank into the cold snow, which didn't feel cold. Naked, they rolled and yelled in the whiteness until their bodies cooled. That day she decided she'd marry him.

"That's it for me," says Wes. Liza likes being able to endure the heat as long as Wes. It's just been in the last five years that she can do this.

He runs and jumps into the water. Liza goes down the three cement steps to the creek and, without stopping, dives head-first in the opposite direction. For a moment, her body seems to shut down, to actually absorb the blackness that is underwater. In the next second, she is stunned by reaching what feels like the brilliant peak of an icy mountain.

She comes up and screams at the shock. Wes does the same next to her. The creek has carried her to him.

On shore, Liza is not cold. Every part of her body feels smoothed of wrinkles and imperfections. As many times as she and Wes have taken sauna, Liza never quite expects what comes next: the pause that first makes her so light she nearly leaves the ground, and then descends to hold her and Wes together, in place.

People cannot be witnesses to enduring romance, but this ritual, this sauna, can.

Wes and Liza stand facing the creek. Behind them, in dark holes plants are coming to life. The fire burns on. Clouds of vapor float off Wes and Liza; every pore of their flushed bodies breathes. A piece of house siding floats by and, unmoving, they watch its determined journey. A wild duck skids along the stream surface making two straight lines with its feet. The lines repeat themselves in small separate waves and then blend into one moment.

Gypsies

The first time she heard the sound, she worked it into the office scene she was dreaming about. The noise transformed into tiny staples pinging around her desk. Uniform bits of metal hit her lamp, her bulletin board, the computer screen and telephone as she groped for the electric stapler silently punching away, out of control.

Lately her dreams, the ones she remembered anyway, have all had to do with work. Without opening her eyes, Lynn raised up on one elbow, pulled the window shut, then settled back into bed and turned away from her husband. "Rain," she whispered.

In the morning she stood on the porch of their cedar-sided Cape and surveyed the surrounding acres for evidence of a shower. But the ground was as dry and hard as the slabs of shale leading from the driveway to their front door; the grass was browning in patches; the thick summer leaves were dull. The dark peppering on the walkway seemed to be some kind of seed or pollen from the huge northern white oak, which stood less than fifteen feet from the front door. Extending well above the roof of the house, the tree's lower trunk was visible from the living room window, and its leafy branches could be seen from the bedroom. Lynn regarded the oak as an integral part of the house. Sort of the way her job as a computer trainer had come to identify her when she met someone for the first time.

Two years earlier, when Lynn had asked the realtor why anyone would plant a tree so close to a house, Mrs. Goodhue had responded that the tree was far older than the Connecticut house.

"You mean someone actually planned a house around the tree?" As Mrs. Goodhue shrugged at Lynn's question, Lynn had quickly asked another, "Don't they wrap their roots around your pipes?" From childhood, Lynn remembered her grandparents' scarred front lawn caused by the removal of a weeping willow, and the panicked reaction of neighbors convinced that trees could squeeze a house dry. The result had been blocks scraped clear of any growth over four feet tall.

As Mrs. Goodhue explained that there were no pipes in the front of the house, Joe said gently, "It's good protection. It shades the house in summer, breaks up the winds in winter." From then on, when she pointed out space-saving wall units, effective lighting, and double-pane windows, Mrs. Goodhue spoke directly to Joe.

"We'll take the tree. I mean, the house," Joe had said to Mrs. Goodhue.

The tree was a joke for months as Joe and Lynn made household purchases. "I'll take the tree," one or the other of them said with every acquisition—couch, chairs, lamps, a juicer, an electric can opener, a food processor, a microwave oven, an espresso maker, a compact disk player, a personal computer for Lynn, who brought work home from the office.

At first, Lynn had thought the three-bedroom, two-bath house was too big for the two of them.

"You've got to be kidding," Joe had said. "In a couple of months we're not going to have room for a fax machine."

"Who has a fax machine?" Lynn had asked.

But Joe's prediction came true. The way they filled the house made Lynn remember how, as a young girl, she'd grown into new, larger dresses stashed at the back of her closet. The blank white walls and echoes of Joe and Lynn's voices quickly disappeared as they bought devices, decorations, and furnishings, and, after last year's raise, a fitness center. Despite all the acquisitions to make their personal and professional lives easier, faster, smoother, Joe and Lynn worked harder than ever.

"Aren't you going to work today?" Joe asked as he kissed her hurriedly on the way to the car. After the red Miata had disappeared down the driveway, she was still thinking about the VCR Plus they'd bought the night before. Before going to bed they'd argued about programming it, then over the best place to put it. Lately they seemed to go through a similar irksome ritual with every purchase, especially if it had to be assembled.

Most days Lynn simply fell into the routine of preparing for work, working, unwinding from work. But once in a while, particularly on mornings like this one, she'd feel a moment or two of clarity, like that which came with the fresh air after a rainstorm. She'd see that she and Joe spent too much time trying to pay their mortgage, accumulate luxuries. At first it had been a challenge, an exciting responsibility. But now the daily, obligatory rhythm of working—he in liquor sales, she in computers—and spending had become like lifting weights or running. They couldn't stop.

Since Joe had been promoted to department head the previous year, he worked even longer hours. Before the raise, he'd said if he could only make sales head he could finally relax. Now, their vacations were the bonus trips Joe earned for having the best sales figures in the tri-state area.

Lynn didn't want Joe to become too ambitious. Her first husband had been so driven he'd starting carrying a toothbrush in the pocket protector permanently attached to his shirt.

Everyone had said she and Ben, with their fair coloring, light hair, and sharply defined features, looked more like siblings than spouses. Sometimes she forgot about the exciting change it had been to marry Joe, who was a good foot taller than she was, three years older, and with dark reddish hair and a softness about his features.

———⋈———

The sound she imagined was rain woke Lynn all week except for Friday night, after a Valium. That day had been particularly trying. She was training an insurance company's employees on their new system. The questions erupting from the gray and tan jackets and pale shirts had made Lynn dizzy. Half were paranoiac (What are the early warning signs of a computer virus?), the other half adolescent (What I want to know is how you make this "genius" light your cigarette).

Joe suggested she unwind by watching one of the eight movies he'd taped that week, but she was too tired.

Saturday morning the ground around their house was still dry. The specks of black spattered along the walkway had doubled in size and number since she'd first noticed them.

"It's crap," Joe said as she swept.

When she looked up at him, she saw a caterpillar dangling by an invisible thread from the tree. "Yuck," she said and moved out of its way only to find a second one near her left hand.

"What's going on?" she asked Joe, who was examining a dark line moving up a supporting post of the house.

"Must be gypsy moth caterpillars," Joe said. "I heard somebody talking about it at the gas station last night. The caterpillars are supposed to be pretty bad this year." He said the sound she thought was rain was caterpillars defecating as they ate the oak leaves.

"You'd be able to hear that?" Lynn asked.

"Sure, if there were a thousand caterpillars all doing it together." He walked toward her. "Here's some new ones." He pointed out a Dijon mustard–colored egg mass broken open and discharging a mass of tiny wrigglers.

Lynn thought that Joe must have gotten *some* biology lesson at the gas station. "Well," she said softly, looking at the darkened walkway, "at least it's not a weird atmospheric thing."

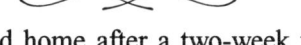

When Lynn returned home after a two-week training session in Chicago, the trees surrounding their house showed signs of damage, especially the great oak. Its leaves were fringed, and bits of uneaten leaves littered the lawn.

"It looks like fall has chewed its way here," Lynn said, although October was four months off. She'd considered passing up the trip, but in the end decided that she and Joe could use the extra travel allowance.

"Oaks are their favorites," Joe offered. He handed her a Tanqueray and tonic, and gave her a peck on the cheek.

Lynn picked up the library book on insect pests. "Does it say how long these things last?" she asked.

"I haven't gotten to that part yet," Joe said. From the electronics catalog in his hand, she saw that he'd been distracted.

As they sat and drank on the porch in the near dark, Joe said, "It's hard to imagine this house without the tree."

She took a couple swallows of the drink and softened. "It's hard to believe we really own these trees, isn't it?" Before he could respond, she said, "I mean, trees just don't seem to be things you can own like cars and clothes and chairs and lawn mowers. Speaking of that . . ."

"You're right," he said. "I'll cut the grass tomorrow."

Maintaining the lawn was a sizable job. Joe routinely cut, while she trimmed around the rock gardens and bushes. They didn't bother with pruning or fertilizing or composting or gardening. Just cutting the massive lawn was outdoor activity enough for them.

"Imagine that the house was built as a tribute to the tree," Lynn said, feeling a little woozy after her second drink.

"Why? Because so many of its brothers and sisters had to be killed for it to be built?"

"You know what I mean," she said.

"I don't think I do," he said and went inside. "You always start talking weird when you've been away from home," he called.

"And you always go shopping," she called back.

After she'd unpacked and gotten into bed, she decided that the raining sound the insects made had definitely become louder. She was sure of it.

"You can sleep through anything," Lynn accused Joe.

"Thank you," he said. "But not this." He grabbed her around the waist, but she pulled away from him.

"Joe, I'm exhausted."

"I guess I am, too," he said, almost apologetically.

In the next weeks, the caterpillars grew thick and fat as baby fingers. The opulent pulsating lengths ambled up the cracks in the oak bark to eat what remained of its leaves, and lowered themselves back to the ground on barely visible threads when they were through. Their nightly feasting sounds became louder than a drizzle. The noise grew so disturbing that even when the nights were cool, Lynn closed the window and turned on the air conditioner.

She put a light blanket on the bed and pulled Joe's arm around her. Awake from the purr of machinery, she pictured the tree, which had acquired the presence of a person. Now it was an old person, like her grandfather when he'd gotten leukemia and ever so gradually left her.

She imagined the caterpillars' appetite spreading past the oak and the line of trees protecting her house from her neighbors, then into the forest. Joe had recently told her about acres of forest land in New York state that had been defoliated a couple of years earlier. Summer had quickly changed to winter, without the brilliant transition of autumn.

She and Joe had changed just as drastically. They both had histories of moving from apartment to apartment, job to job. They'd both been married before. They'd suddenly settled in Connecticut and found themselves working long hours. Their possessions had grown so numerous that Lynn felt not nestled in place but cemented.

She could sense that Joe hadn't fallen asleep either. "What about spraying?" she whispered.

"Too close to the well," he said so quickly that she knew he'd already considered it.

Lynn walked up the crushed stone driveway to her neighbor's house to deliver a UPS package. She ran her hand through her hair in case a stray caterpillar had dropped there. Before knocking on Mrs. Hoyt's door, Lynn scraped her shoes clean of squashed caterpillars.

Joe and Lynn had spoken to Elizabeth Hoyt only a couple of times in the nearly two years they'd lived next door. The

Connecticut town was populated by newcomers—commuters to New York City or retirees who'd once summered or spent weekends in Connecticut—and old-time New Englanders whose relatives had established the town. Mrs. Hoyt belonged to the latter camp, which frequently commented about the prices newcomers paid for their homes.

Standing in the doorway of her neat white house, devoid of even a window box or wind chimes, the white-haired woman wore such a plain, dark dress that Lynn wanted to call her Goody Hoyt.

Joe said Mrs. Hoyt was a stingy old bat who was tight with everything—even her words. Lynn, too, had never heard the woman utter more than a few sentences. But today Mrs. Hoyt seemed almost chatty when Lynn handed over the package.

"Oh good, my drugs," the old woman volunteered. "Blood pressure medicine," she said and winked. "It's half what I used to pay that bandit Minero." Minero owned the local pharmacy.

Lynn looked beyond Mrs. Hoyt into the living room. The room was spare. No photographs or artwork adorned the walls, no vases or art books rested on the two low tables. Joe and Lynn's leather love seats would be extravagantly out of place at Mrs. Hoyt's. Lynn imagined the woman's closets packed with old paper bags, pieces of string, aluminum pie pans. Yet this bare-bones house stood less than 500 feet from Lynn's own.

"Spray yet?" Mrs. Hoyt coughed.

"No, but we did get these traps to catch the moths before they mate."

Mrs. Hoyt shook her head. "That's fine for next year. Doesn't solve the problem now, though." She pointed to four immense trees spread across her front lawn. A band of burlap encircled each one about four-and-a-half feet above its base.

"In the evening they start climbing up the trees so they can eat all night. You've likely heard them," Mrs. Hoyt said. Lynn rolled her eyes. "The burlap deters them. Temporarily anyway. Gives you a chance to pick them off."

Lynn followed Mrs. Hoyt out to the trees. With a stick, the woman lifted the overhanging lip of the burlap securely tied to the tree. Masses of caterpillars clung to its underside.

"God," Lynn said. "How disgusting."

Mrs. Hoyt cleared her throat. "May be. But if this keeps up, we'll be seeing a lot more of each other." Using the stick as a pointer, Mrs. Hoyt indicated the border of beeches between their houses. The protective row of foliage, which, in summer, normally made Mrs. Hoyt's house invisible, had become flimsy as a veil.

"She said tape would work, too," Lynn advised as she held a twig to the first chubby caterpillar delayed on the tape girdling their oak. The insect swung its head, its antennae right and left. She quickly flicked it into an old mayonnaise jar half full of kerosene.

"Reminds me of getting Japanese beetles when we were kids," Joe said from the other side of the tree.

"I don't think she even owns a TV," Lynn said.

"Mrs. Hoyt?"

"Uh huh."

"Is that possible?" Joe asked. "Doesn't everybody own a TV?"

Lynn didn't answer but thought of the old woman who did everything herself—cleaning and canning and painting.

"She seems self-sufficient," Lynn said, a hint of admiration in her voice.

"Masochistic is more like it," Joe said.

As Lynn deterred the caterpillars from their destructive mission, she remembered that in two days she'd have to be in Boston to train a magazine staff. She picked and flicked the caterpillars; her jar grew dark with the squirming bodies. Compulsive eaters, they seemed to grow fatter by the day. They went after food so blindly they'd strain against any obstacle, sometimes leaving bits of themselves behind in their struggle toward more feasting.

A few brownish gypsy moths fluttered overhead in search of females, white and unable to fly. The week before, in the crevices of the oak, Lynn had spotted some of the caterpillars in the pupa stage spinning themselves into sticky white gobs.

When it was nearly dark, Joe and Lynn held up their containers. "I got more," Joe said.

Joe began arriving home by four-thirty instead of six so that he had plenty of time to "harvest" the caterpillars before dusk. Instead of playing nightly computer games, Joe worked with Lynn on the tree and talked over the workday.

"Be careful not to let the caterpillars touch your skin," Joe said. "It kind of has a numbing effect."

"Don't worry about that," Lynn said, though she was curious to poke one of the pests.

"I wish the birds did a better job of eating these things," Lynn said. Minutes before, Joe had put his jar down and clapped when a bird plucked a large caterpillar from a branch.

"There aren't that many birds," Joe said.

"Do you think the caterpillars make a bird's mouth numb?" she asked.

"I don't know the first thing about a bird's mouth, Lynn," he said and laughed. He proceeded to reveal how he'd caught a chipmunk one summer when his family spent their vacation in Pennsylvania. He told Lynn he'd cried when they made him let it go.

"I've never heard this story before," Lynn said gently and put her arm around him.

"I'd forgotten it until now," he said.

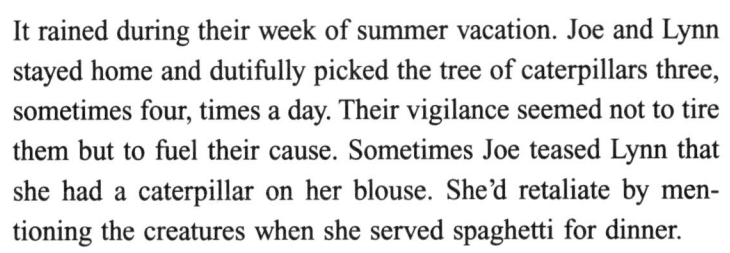

It rained during their week of summer vacation. Joe and Lynn stayed home and dutifully picked the tree of caterpillars three, sometimes four, times a day. Their vigilance seemed not to tire them but to fuel their cause. Sometimes Joe teased Lynn that she had a caterpillar on her blouse. She'd retaliate by mentioning the creatures when she served spaghetti for dinner.

Even with all their efforts, some of the caterpillars survived, and the tree's greenery continued to disappear. The oak became lacy, the yard under it eerily lit by sunshine where previously shade had spread. The effect reminded Lynn of a room without curtains, like their bedroom when they'd first moved in.

"I think we've lost it," Joe said softly as he screwed the lid on his mayonnaise jar. He sighed. "It's going to cost an arm and a leg to get this damn tree taken down."

Joe hadn't been so despondent since six months earlier when an entire shipment of Jack Daniel's had arrived at his warehouse damaged.

"Joe, let's get away from this, at least for the weekend," Lynn suggested. She was surprised when he agreed.

For two days they went to museums and movies in New York, never venturing near Central Park and its trees. They held hands in restaurants and on buses, bracing themselves against what was happening at home.

On their return Sunday evening, the yard was oddly quiet. No familiar pinging on the leaves. In the darkness, Lynn wondered: maybe there are no more leaves. Maybe in the couple of days that she and Joe had been away, the entire forest behind the house had disappeared.

"Want to pick off a few gypsies before we go in?" Joe joked as he shut the car door.

"Nature works in mysterious ways," Mrs. Hoyt called out from her porch.

"What?" asked Joe, hollering back.

Lynn walked toward the oak. The timed exterior lights of their house had come on, illuminating the giant tree as if it were a monument. She stood at the tree and stared at hundreds, thousands of caterpillars in soft upside-down Vs and Us caught in the rough bark. There were so many, they looked like a pattern on the tree, a tweed.

"Joe, they're all dead."

Joe rested his hand on her shoulder. "I can't believe it," he said, studying the soft curved lines of blackness. "They look like hooks, or bent nails or something."

"Probably an aerial spraying," Lynn said.

"The blight," Mrs. Hoyt said behind them. Her white hair made a thick, wild halo against the dark. A little out of breath, she told them about the fungus that had grown strong during the recent rains and killed the caterpillars.

"Are you sure you didn't spring for a chemical dusting, Mrs. Hoyt?" Joe teased.

"Not me," she said, turning to leave. "Read the paper. It's all there."

"Too bad the fungus didn't show up a month ago," Joe said, loud enough for her to hear.

"Don't look a gift horse in the mouth," Mrs. Hoyt said.

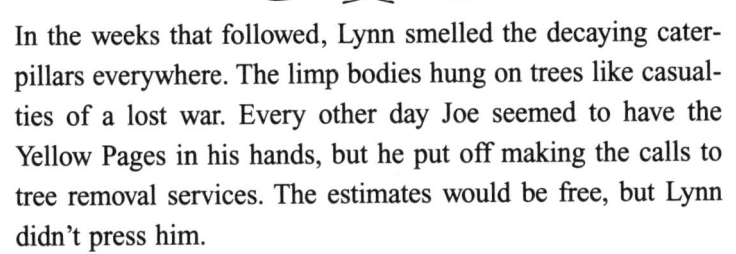

In the weeks that followed, Lynn smelled the decaying caterpillars everywhere. The limp bodies hung on trees like casualties of a lost war. Every other day Joe seemed to have the Yellow Pages in his hands, but he put off making the calls to tree removal services. The estimates would be free, but Lynn didn't press him.

Then one day, as she was changing the sheets on the water bed, she saw something unusual against the stark brown limbs of the oak. She squinted, then moved up close to the window, raised the screen, and looked out.

"Joe," she screamed. "You won't believe this."

"No more damn caterpillars," Joe said.

Tiny leaves, the green of April, were just starting to unfurl. A second growth.

That night after dinner they sat out on the porch in front of the tree with glasses of Chardonnay. A few gypsy moths that had struggled out of their cocoons before the fungus took over fluttered around like torn pieces of paper.

"More gypsies," Lynn said, eyeing the moths nervously. She knew they were mating and searching for safe places to lay their yellowish masses of eggs, which would hatch next year.

"Don't worry about them," Joe said. "There's too few to make any difference. It'll be years before they build up their forces again."

Joe led Lynn to the oak. He kissed her, and they dropped to the ground as hungrily as the mating deer she'd once spotted behind the house.

Lynn felt herself slipping back to five years earlier when she'd met Joe at a bar. It was before either of them owned a car or used a fax machine or had tasted focaccia. She'd been mesmerized by his dark red hair and blue eyes and by the way he rested his forearm in front of him like a barrier against his feelings.

Joe kissed her again. Wasn't this—just this union—what they really were working so hard for?

She looked up into the sky, conscious that, even as she watched, the oak's web of branches was bearing new leaves. A light rain touched her face. She felt it on her eyes and arms and fingers as she reached for Joe and pulled him to her.

The Blue Room

*C*heryl stood on the newly painted porch of a white house in Chesterville and tried to sell herself to the owner. Although Cheryl's long, sandy-colored hair stripped five years from her age, thirty-three, she wasn't sure that was enough. Mrs. Terke seemed to prefer boarders who hadn't yet been touched by difficulty. The old woman for sure wouldn't want to hear about a separation.

Mrs. Terke said that ever since her husband died, she'd rented the two bedrooms on the second floor to young women attending St. John's College. Mrs. Terke stared off and reminisced. "There was a darling girl. I think her name was Katrina. She majored in music. Just darling."

Mrs. Terke put her finger to her lower lip and looked back at Cheryl, who felt as if her every thought and ambition were distorted by the woman's thick glasses. Cheryl sensed she was being searched for naïveté, for innocence, for blind enthusiasm—qualities she couldn't remember ever having. Such characteristics wouldn't take up any space in a small bedroom in a small house, or light up its walls and ceiling at all hours of the night, or set its floorboards moaning with her pacing.

"I *am* planning to take classes," Cheryl said. She'd thought about that possibility only minutes before as she'd walked by the college. Mrs. Terke sighed and placed her index finger back against her lip as if daring herself to reply.

"This is such a perfect house," Cheryl said softly, careful to say "house" instead of "location." The residence was almost equidistant from St. John's College and Merry Woods, a nursing home where Cheryl had, just two hours before, gotten a job as an aide. Although some of the patients there didn't seem any older than Mrs. Terke, they'd lost interest in their appearance. It wasn't Sunday, but Mrs. Terke was dressed as if she were on her way to church. She wore lipstick and clip-on earrings, a pleasant perfume, not too heavily applied, and a delicately flowered dress.

When Cheryl had originally boarded the bus in Baltimore, she'd planned to take it all the way into Delaware, to Beauville, on the shore, where years earlier she'd gone on her senior class trip. Beauville was all she knew of this side of the Chesapeake Bay, and she remembered the morning there, when the sun rose red over the Atlantic and hundreds of white butterflies flickered above the hills of sand.

But about an hour and a half before the bus was scheduled to reach Beauville, Cheryl had noticed signs for Chesterville, Maryland. And just as she made the connection between the town that had been in the TV news for the last couple of weeks and this actual village a few miles from the gentle shore of the Chesapeake Bay, she heard the comments of the bus driver and a few passengers around her.

"That's the place," the driver had said, pointing to a sign indicating a seven after the town's name.

A woman ahead of Cheryl shook her head and groaned in disgust.

When Cheryl had first heard about the strange man who

stalked the college town, mugged young women, and then cut off pieces of their hair, she guessed the assailant was some disgruntled boyfriend who wanted to mark the women who'd refused him. Ed, her husband, had told her to stop acting like a psychiatrist.

"Could it be some kind of fraternity thing?" Cheryl asked the driver. She'd heard the stories: guys who drank unbelievable amounts of beer by holding funnels to their mouths.

"Nope," said the bus driver with conviction. He looked at Cheryl through his rearview mirror. "The police say this fellah is a professional. He's likely got a record." The driver looked back at the road. "Besides, there's no fraternities at St. John's."

"A man like that is just marking time," a woman across from Cheryl said. "Getting ready to . . ." The woman paused and Cheryl watched her searching for a euphemism for rape. "To do something really horrible," the woman said as she turned and stared at Cheryl's hair hanging loose below her shoulders. "How far are you going, honey?" the woman asked.

"Beauville."

"Beauville's a lovely town," the woman answered.

As relief spread across the woman's motherly face, Cheryl wondered whether it would be more exciting or more terrifying to live in a place where an unknown man had been dubbed the "Chesterville Barber." She considered how she might change in a town she knew absolutely nothing about except for brief, ominous clips on television.

The driver downshifted as he approached Chesterville's Main Street, and the bus bellowed past the neat, silent houses and small storefronts. The town seemed as unlikely to be extraordinary as Cheryl's marriage had. There were no video cameras or television news crews visible. The residents didn't appear to be homebound in terror. She spotted a "Help Wanted" sign at Merry Woods, just before the bus pulled into a gas station where two passengers waited to board. Before they could get on, Cheryl gathered her belongings and hurried off the bus. She walked toward the nursing home without turning to wave at the confused passengers.

"I'm quiet," Cheryl said, but Mrs. Terke remained unmoved. Cheryl wasn't normally so insistent, but every time she thought of Ed telling her what she could and couldn't do she was propelled into action.

"I'm very neat," Cheryl persisted, though she was pushing the truth. "Neat" was not an adjective Ed would have used for her.

"This place looks like a dump," he'd said to her at least once a week for most of the fourteen years they'd been married. That was one of the things Cheryl missed about Ed—his regular expressions, which while they had lost their edge over time, still served to remind her of who she was.

"I'm . . . ," Cheryl almost pleaded as she searched for a characteristic that Mrs. Terke would find appropriate. But in the end she didn't know what to say that wasn't a lie.

"If I haven't found a college girl by Saturday, the room is yours. Thirty dollars a week in advance. Cash," Mrs. Terke said, widening her eyes at the word "cash."

As Cheryl turned to go, Mrs. Terke said, "I suppose I don't have to tell you, the first incident happened just two streets away."

―――

The inside of the house matched its crisp white exterior and tidy, painted porch. Cheryl noticed the spotless walls and highly polished furniture, the soft area rugs centered on shiny hardwood floors. The bedroom Cheryl rented was small and blue, smelled of lemon wax, and featured an ensemble in walnut: a single bed, nightstand, dresser, and desk.

Cheryl sat on the edge of the bed and ate from a large bag of fried chicken. Although she was more than two hours from her old home in Baltimore, with the wide expanse of the bay in between, in a room with little trace of her, Cheryl did not feel truly hidden. She imagined the aroma of greasy chicken following her up the steps and into this room where Ed could find her if he set his mind to it.

The bathroom on the other side of the hall was larger than Cheryl's blue bedroom. The toilet and sink sat at some distance from the huge, claw-foot bathtub. Cheryl carefully washed chicken grease from her hands and face. There was no shower, so Cheryl knelt in the tub and washed her head under its faucet. Leaning back on her feet, she lathered and rubbed at her head, then rinsed under the thick stream of water. By the time she'd flushed every bit of soap from her long hair, her arms ached.

Cheryl hadn't cut her hair in the fourteen years she'd been married to Ed. He used to gather it up in his hand, tight against her head, and say that he wished he had such healthy, thick hair. Then he'd pull her head back a little roughly and kiss her on the neck. Sometimes his determination aroused her, but more and more, the way he tugged made her feel like a marionette. Lately, though, he hadn't touched her much. It was as if fingering her hair reminded him of the widening circle of bare scalp on his own head.

Cheryl felt uncharacteristically self-conscious standing in the middle of the large room to dry her body. She wasn't used to so much space between herself and other things. In the bathroom of the apartment she'd shared with Ed there wasn't room to bend over without bumping into some fixture. And yet, one night after they'd had a few too many beers, Ed had trailed her into the bathroom when she turned on the shower, and squeezed into the compartment with her. One or the other of them kept crashing against the shower's metal sides, the hollow thunder pressing them closer and making them laugh. While Cheryl remembered that incident with Ed as one of the good times, she couldn't help but recall, too, the feeling of tightness—other people pushing her and Ed up against each other, pressing all their possessions into one tiny one-bedroom after another. Everything so confined until, after a while, she couldn't tell who was doing the pushing.

When Cheryl finished in the bathroom, and the steamy air followed her out to dust the hall mirror, Cheryl could hear the other boarder, Mindy, talking excitedly to Mrs. Terke.

The news drifted up the staircase: a sophomore walking the dimly lit path between the biology building and the library had been attacked. The young woman was grabbed from behind, her hands bound, and then her long hair cut and reduced to uneven stubble. Almost as an afterthought, the victim's pocket money, seven dollars, had been stolen.

Cheryl heard the dead bolt slide into position on the front door. Lying on the single bed and studying the bare blue walls for any hint of previous boarders or of Mrs. Terke's younger son, Tommy, who'd grown up in the room, Cheryl listened to Mindy preparing for a date. Mindy opened and closed windows and closets in the large bedroom with the double bed that had once belonged to Mrs. Terke's firstborn son. Mindy seemed merely to dress and sleep in the spacious room next to Cheryl's. All day Mindy attended classes at St. John's, and evenings she spent with Dominic, a handsome, clean-cut young man who was overly polite to Mrs. Terke. Mindy was petite, not even reaching Dominic's shoulders, but otherwise the two looked enough alike to be twins. Ed had been a foot taller than Cheryl and a hundred pounds heavier, and everyone said right from the day they were introduced that they didn't look as if they went together.

Most nights Cheryl was awakened by Mindy coming up the stairs. Listening to the steps' continuous grumble, Cheryl felt comfortable in her new bed. She had always shared a bed—with one, sometimes two, of her sisters; with a number of different roommates from work; with her husband. The only time in her life she'd ever had a bed to herself was when she'd been sick at home. Then, she had been assigned a cot against one of the walls of the living room. Her mother would periodically place her wide palm against Cheryl's forehead, then against her own, to check for a temperature, and dutifully deliver drinks and soups. From the cot, Cheryl could watch TV until late at night. Being ill was the only time she had felt indulged.

Cheryl pulled her arms up close to her chest. Her damp hair made a mark against the pillow. Even though it was August, she felt a chill when a breeze, like the whisper of a stranger, passed in through the open window.

After a week at Mrs. Terke's, Cheryl discovered that her initial observation about her landlady's fastidiousness was incorrect. While the house was spotless—the legs of the chairs around the large mahogany table carefully fitted to indentations on the rug, and every piece of mail aligned in a tidy stack by the phone—personally Mrs. Terke was obsessed with aberration. She permitted only impeccable girls to be boarders, but her fascination anchored on those who deviated from her standards.

Like many old people Cheryl knew, once Mrs. Terke got onto

a topic she wouldn't let it go. In this respect, she seemed as tenacious as the notorious stalker. Every day, Mrs. Terke asked Mindy if she knew any more about the girl who'd been attacked. And after a woman who wasn't a college student fell victim to the mugger, Mrs. Terke approached Cheryl.

Cheryl began to imagine that Mrs. Terke lay in wait for her, that each time she or Mindy entered the house, Mrs. Terke checked them out. Mindy was searched for news, statistics, gossip. Cheryl was asked in private to respond to Mrs. Terke's larger curiosities such as, "Why do you suppose he chose that particular young lady for his victim?"

Cheryl spent a lot of time in her small blue room, trying to figure things out. How Ed was getting on without her; if he'd given up looking for her. She thought about the attacker who took hair as his prize. She'd heard once that some people committed crimes to feel that rush of being alive. Then she thought of the original resident of the blue room—Tommy. The only thing she knew about Mrs. Terke's son was his name.

"It's a shame," Mrs. Terke said, shaking her head one evening after she'd heard about yet another victim. This woman had not only had her hair drastically cut and her money stolen—bus fare for a weekend in Ocean City—but she'd also been beaten. There was some question whether the attacker had actually been responsible for her cuts and bruises; the woman had a history of spousal abuse.

"Have you eaten yet?" Mrs. Terke asked Cheryl. "Well, then, how about a TV dinner? I've got an extra chicken you're more than welcome to."

Cheryl was moved that Mrs. Terke, who must have once served elaborate meals to a roomful of guests at her mahogany table, was now eating TV dinners alone in the kitchen.

"Call me Patrice," Mrs. Terke said, as Cheryl's crossed arms settled on the kitchen table's worn oilcloth covering.

"Patrice," Cheryl repeated, incredulous that the French name could possibly belong to Mrs. Terke.

One morning and two evenings a week now, Cheryl took French classes at St. John's College. She'd thought at first of telling Mrs. Terke that she was studying sociology, which would be more consistent with working in a nursing home. But Mrs. Terke might notice her textbooks. In the end, Cheryl simply said she was working on her liberal arts degree, an ambition Mrs. Terke approved of.

To Cheryl, French, with its beautiful, strange sounds, epitomized the exotic. Something Ed would be baffled by. Yet Ed had been the one to give her the idea about two years ago. They'd been having a fight, and Ed had said out of the blue, "That makes as much sense as me studying French." Cheryl couldn't remember now what that fight had been about. She was never sure what she and Ed fought about, but just before she'd left Baltimore, they had seemed to be in a constant quarrel that often elevated to screams. At the end she couldn't pin the fault of their arguments on one or the other, as she could when they'd first married.

"I sure hope they catch that fellow," Mrs. Terke said as she retrieved the aluminum pans from the oven.

Cheryl peeled back the hot foil covering her dinner, and a burst of heat hit her in the face.

"So," Mrs. Terke said when she turned from Cheryl to the coffeepot. "No boyfriends for you?" Mrs. Terke's voice sounded not so much prying as compassionate. It often did when she and Cheryl were alone. The hot, soft chicken pieces coaxed Cheryl into forgetting how the woman patronized her.

Cheryl shook her head and cut the chicken with her fork. Her wedding ring now lay among the coins in the change purse of her wallet. Since she'd been in Chesterville, Cheryl had avoided mentioning Ed; he didn't fit into this house. Yet she knew that details of Ed were precisely what would capture Mrs. Terke's imagination.

Ed had walked out many times, returning a couple of days later, all apologetic and ready to start over. But after the last fight, he came back to an empty apartment. Cheryl liked to imagine his reaction when he searched their living room, kitchen, bathroom, bedroom, until finally her name became a question, not a command.

"I'm separated," Cheryl said. Mrs. Terke's fork stopped clicking against the foil pan.

"I see," said Mrs. Terke.

"We agreed on a separation," Cheryl said, unwilling to tell the old woman that she'd finally just walked out. Walked away from the dull apartment where their possessions ran together, walked down the street she knew so well and now remembered so little.

Cheryl knew that lots of people liked routine. But predictability made her claustrophobic. Perhaps nothing would alter a person's workday short of quitting, but somehow she'd always hoped her marriage would surmount the bland wash of mediocrity. Yet life with Ed had gotten so familiar that she knew which words he'd emphasize in his sentences. Sometimes she thought of their bed as an endless field, its corn already harvested, the stalks shorn down to rough stubble for as far as she could see.

The only thing that changed the expected was their fights, which Cheryl now found hard to distinguish. Had she insti-

The Blue Room

gated trouble simply to keep from dropping off into a fog of boredom?

"He's not going to be showing up here in the middle of the night beating at my door, is he?" the widow asked. Mrs. Terke watched two and a half hours of soap operas every day.

Without looking up, Cheryl again shook her head.

"You don't walk by yourself in the evenings, do you?" Mrs. Terke's sudden concern disoriented Cheryl. She wasn't sure if the interest was sincere or if Mrs. Terke was nurturing a real-life soap opera in her own home.

Cheryl said that she didn't, that she met up with her friends. But in truth she had no friends among the sour, resigned aides at the nursing home, or among the young, privileged students who had time for tennis and music lessons in addition to classes. When Cheryl was the age of her classmates, she was already married, working at a butcher's booth in Lexington Market and, at night, trying to get pregnant.

"Just don't flaunt that hair of yours," came Mrs. Terke's advice. "I'd wear a hat if I were you." Mrs. Terke pushed back from the kitchen table and cleared away the empty frozen-dinner pans.

Indian summer evenings in Chesterville were no time for hats. The air was so still and thick that Cheryl imagined herself walking through layers of curtains, which parted ever so slightly for a body to pass. Insects mumbled like applause as Cheryl made her way to the college, French words coming to her, their foreign syllables making her feel momentarily important—*petite, grande, enfant.* In French, even "husband" was transformed into a lovely sound—*mari.*

On Sunday evening Cheryl and Mrs. Terke were watching the evening news when Mindy and Dominic burst into the room with a hysterical young woman. As soon as the girl lowered her hands from her head, Cheryl realized what had happened.

"Right here, Darlene," Mindy said, directing her to the sofa.

Darlene's face was blotchy from crying, and half of her hair had been cut in a jagged, close crop. Most of the baby-fine hair on the left side of her face hung freely to her shoulders. It appeared that she'd literally torn herself away from her attacker. For the first time, Cheryl considered that the mugger might be someone desperate for something to call his own, even if it was only a designation as the Chesterville Barber.

Darlene sobbed while Mrs. Terke made tea and Dominic and Mindy called the police.

The girl's hands were small and childlike, the fingernails bitten. She looked only about sixteen, but Mindy said Darlene was a sophomore like herself. Mindy softly explained how she and Dominic had interrupted the attack.

Mrs. Terke's hand shook when she set the tea and a shot of apple brandy on the coffee table in front of Darlene. "There you go, dear," Mrs. Terke said and patted Darlene's shoulder. The girl flinched, then smiled weakly.

"Did he do anything . . . ," Mrs. Terke cleared her throat, "sexual, dear?" Darlene stopped crying, shook her head.

"You don't have to say anything if you don't want to. Not before the police get here," Cheryl offered.

Mrs. Terke glared at Cheryl. In her navy blue dress, Mrs. Terke reminded Cheryl of a large dark bird watching a scene of carnage from a distance, but ready to swoop down for the remains.

"I had exactly a dollar and a quarter on me," the young woman said finally.

"Pervert," Mindy said.

"Did you get a look at his face?" Mrs. Terke asked. Darlene explained that the tall man had been wearing a stocking over his head.

"The guy's a sicko," Dominic said, winding his arm around Mindy's waist. Cheryl missed Ed's thick arm at her side at that moment, though she was doing OK without the rest of him.

"At least . . ." Cheryl started to say softly, more to console herself that rape wasn't part of the attacker's plan than to comfort Darlene. Then, as if to convince them all that something irreplaceable *had* been taken from her, Darlene began to cry harder.

Cheryl had cried that way at the altar. She had bit the inside of her mouth and refused to look at Ed. But then fear rushed out of her, and Ed looked away, embarrassed, as the minister comforted her and helped her compose herself. Afterward, at the reception, while everyone clinked knives to glasses to coax the two to kiss, Ed had covered her hand with his large one and said gently, "I'll take care of you. Don't worry." And then, as she closed her eyes and kissed him at the noisy insistence of other couples all around her, she saw every candle at the altar flicker and go out.

"Be careful here alone," Mrs. Terke warned. She was going to a family reunion in Virginia. Since Mindy and Dominic had brought Darlene to the house the week before, one more coed and a supermarket cashier had been attacked and gagged, had their hair cut to a ragged stubble, and then been robbed of their pocket change by a tall man with a stocking stretched over his head. The cashier lived three doors down from Mrs. Terke's.

The incidents continued to be reported on the nightly news and in the newspapers, but gradually moved from the lead spot.

Because the nature of the crime hadn't escalated as predicted, even though the number of victims had, the topic was no longer a top priority. And yet it remained a worrisome subject for Cheryl. She found herself thinking weird things about the attacker. For instance, did he keep a collection of hair from his victims hanging on his rearview mirror?

Mrs. Terke hurried through her immaculate rooms and checked last-minute details while her son waited in his car outside the house. He gave a light tap on the horn, which prompted Mrs. Terke to open the front door and signal that she was on her way.

"Tommy's always in a hurry," she said to excuse him. With her son in the vicinity, much of Mrs. Terke's carefully adopted dignity seemed stripped away. Cheryl was curious if Mrs. Terke's dead husband had unbalanced her as easily as Tommy did.

Cheryl wondered if she had anything in common with the man who used to live in the room she now rented. She had imagined that Tommy would be tall and shy. She thought he would ask, "So how do you like the room?" Although the shelves and dresser top in the room were still bare of Cheryl's influence, she was prepared to answer, "It's great," and then for him to add, "Small," as if that were a joke between them. Tommy would have explained what Cheryl already knew—the older brother, Ted, had gotten the large room. Cheryl would have understood perfectly his sense of being shortchanged.

Cheryl had imagined Mrs. Terke saying, "I told him he could move into the big room when Ted went off to college. But he wouldn't have it." And if Tommy asked Cheryl if the room was still blue, Mrs. Terke would surely remark that it wasn't the same blue; the room had been repainted several times.

But today Mrs. Terke wasn't nattering. She was reduced to nervously fixing a brown felt hat over her neat, white bun.

Resting his arms on the hood of his idling Chevy, Tommy looked about fifty. He wasn't tall. He wore sunglasses, and his fair hair was receding. He looked nothing like Mrs. Terke, and didn't appear to be the kind of person to eat in Mrs. Terke's prim dining room. Mrs. Terke had never told Cheryl what Tommy did for a living. From the way he hung on the vehicle as if he were somehow a part of it, occasionally bending to poke a tire or examine the antenna, Cheryl wouldn't have been surprised to hear that Tommy's occupation had to do with cars.

"Be sure to double lock this door tonight. Mindy won't be back until tomorrow, either," Mrs. Terke reminded her.

When Mrs. Terke began to make her way slowly down the porch steps, Tommy didn't come forward to assist her, but hopped back into the car. He reached across the passenger seat and pushed the door open for the old woman as if she were a girl he'd been dating for years.

After the car stuttered off, Cheryl put on a light sweater and sat on the swinging bench on Mrs. Terke's porch. She looked out onto the quiet main street of Chesterville. The house behind her stood firm and warm. Would living here with Ed and a baby have made her happy? She thought of her mother's advice: a child will save your marriage. But her body had refused to save that marriage. Or had it been Ed's?

Recalling the uncharacteristic nervousness of Mrs. Terke as her son waited for her, Cheryl thought for the first time of being old and alone and always on the fringes of being connected. A familiar tightness returned to her throat.

She took a comb out of her sweater pocket and began to stroke her long hair. Electricity crackled through it, and strands clung at the comb as she pulled it free. She combed her hair again and again as the day began to darken. The swing squeaked; her hair crackled from the comb, but no one came to claim her. No one wanted that which comprised her—a husband in Baltimore, a home where old people died when you least expected it, a useless new language.

Maybe Mrs. Terke, now well on her way to Virginia, had wanted something of her. A sensation of panic shot through Cheryl. Had the old woman purposely left her alone to lure excitement right up the porch steps? Or was Mrs. Terke even now relaying her concerns for Cheryl's safety as she and her son drove south? Cheryl would never be sure, but either way, Tommy was turning up the radio instead of listening.

From the day she had moved into Mrs. Terke's house, Cheryl had imagined that something was bound to happen, because for the first time she was living alone, away from her husband of fourteen years, vulnerable because she had long hair. Something or someone would make her cry the way she'd cried the day she'd gotten married. But nothing *had* happened. She walked to work, to class, to Mrs. Terke's house and back every day without being noticed by anyone. Not even when she spoke some French words aloud.

At dusk, Cheryl stuck a few dollars into her jeans pocket. She took a pair of scissors from Mrs. Terke's sewing basket and slid them, point first, into her back pocket. She would make things easy.

She wanted, she needed, some physical proof that she could escape any claim on her. She wouldn't give in as Mrs. Terke had, only to find that even a house and sons couldn't protect her from desperate loneliness.

Cheryl walked toward the campus where so many young women had been frightened and assaulted. She strolled along the quiet paths that sliced through fallen leaves. Her long hair swung out freely, taunting any man with strange ideas in his head. Now and then she stopped, waiting for the sound of other footsteps, for a breath that wasn't the wind.

A rustling startled her, but it was only a squirrel, probably burying acorns he'd soon forget about. Cheryl spun around when a shadow crossed her path. The form turned out to be a broken branch hanging loosely from a large oak.

Perhaps she offered no challenge to the crazy, nameless man. Maybe the man could sense her numbness, her emptiness, and scorn her new recklessness.

Someone was following her. Cheryl began to walk more quickly. The wind picked up and pressed at her face. She began to run. The faster she moved, the more she wanted every old lie torn from her, to forget each job and friend and obligation that she'd had. She didn't even want to speak English anymore. She ran hard, across the wide, sloping lawns between the Arts and Sciences building and the library, then toward the gymnasium. She needed to learn everything in a new way, maybe in French, in anything other than the familiar.

She ran until she fell, exhausted, in a dark spot of leaves and grass. The point of the scissors poked her, reminded her. She pulled them from her pocket and began cutting at her hair. Her hands were strong and determined and out of her control as she hurriedly lifted long bunches of hair and snipped them off. *Mes chevaux.* No. *Mes cheveux.*

Cheryl's hands shook as she scooped up clumps of hair the color of wheat. She gathered every bit of it into a pile, even the wisps stuck to leaves or twigs. In the morning, the evidence, surrounded by expanses of light and blue, would appear to be a fallen nest, abandoned for another that would hold.

The Graveyard

*F*rank sat up in bed when he heard the car horn honk for the second time that night. "Do you know what they call our house?" he asked accusingly.

"Who?" Darla asked sleepily.

"The kids," he said, pointing in the direction of the noise.

"Kids," Darla repeated softly, as if that word explained every difficulty—not just the present disruption by teenagers but Frank and Darla's own grown daughters.

"The graveyard," Frank said accusingly. Even in his frustration, he could see the teenagers' point. A front yard overrun with lawn ornaments resembled a weird burial ground.

Darla had gone overboard. At first, she had simply displayed the toadstools and elves that she'd glazed in her Wednesday ceramics class. Then she'd added the set of life-size bright yellow ducklings.

Frank fed and watered the grass, and grumbled only when he had to mow and trim around his wife's creations. But lately, as the trees had thickened with summer, the things that sprang up on their lawn weren't ceramic; plastic windmills, storks, swans, and flamingos appeared, and wooden girls bent over so that all you saw were chubby legs and ruffled panties. These new decorations held their place on the lawn with long spikes driven deep into the earth. They made Frank think of probes.

Their house was on Route 82, an hour and a half north of New York City. In the thirty years he and Darla had lived there, Frank had kept his lawn and ranch house looking like a model for the development. Then the other day, Bernie Shank had remarked about "gewgaws" on the lawn when Frank had stopped by the convenience store for his regular Lotto ticket.

"Well, so long as the kids don't start parking here and necking," Darla said and turned over.

Darla was proud of her collection. It had started with the traditional black-faced jockey, gloved hand outstretched with a welcoming lantern. The statue had been her mother's, and Darla had taken it when Marlene had gone into the nursing home and the family house was sold. The jockey was the only memento Darla had from the house where she'd been born. She'd gotten Frank to paint the jockey's face white, though, before she set it at the end of her own driveway.

Darla's hobby had grown steadily and included, in addition to the birds and elves, a large white cow with black spots, a donkey in mid kick, a purple frog, and, by the outdoor spigot, a Virgin Mary. She didn't mind that the pieces were all out of proportion—her grazing sheep would have to be ten feet tall to coordinate with the frog's size. Disproportions bothered Frank. A carpenter, he understood about precision in measurements. He liked true-to-life things. When Darla had inserted two yellow and three red wooden tulips along the front of their house, Frank asked, "Why don't you just plant some real flowers, for God's sake?"

To Darla, Frank missed the point. With real flowers you couldn't be sure if they'd come up, what color they'd be, how long they'd display their vibrance before falling away. Plus, in the beginning, you had to wait. With the wooden tulips, there was no chance of disappointment.

In the morning, Darla picked up the empty beer cans flung on the lawn from the night before. She rinsed them and stuck them in a box that Frank would eventually return to the discount beverage store.

Frank was watching the Saturday afternoon ball game when Darla brought out a plate of ham sandwiches and sat beside him. She kept one eye on the game while flipping through a catalog of unusual items for the home. Amid the descriptions of garden hoses painted to resemble snakes, personalized barbecue utensils and aprons, birdhouses customized to the style and color of your actual home, she spotted a couple of lawn ornaments.

"Frank, what do you think of a skunk?"

"What?" he asked without looking up.

"A skunk for the lawn. It's darling," she said, checking the middle of the catalog for shipping charges.

Frank moved his hand in the air between them as if he were swatting an insect. "You've got enough junk out there," he said.

"I don't know why they do all that signaling nonsense," said Darla, referring to the catcher's finger movements at the plate.

"Some things you don't want the world knowing," he said.

During the commercial break, Frank told her he'd heard someone on the pay phone outside the A&P giving directions that used their house as a landmark. "The guy said, 'Take your first right after you pass the house with all the little gnomes. You can't miss it,' " Frank said, thinking that maybe she'd see what he was getting at. It wasn't just him, or simply kids; even adults noticed Darla's excesses.

Frank wouldn't agree, but Darla felt kind of special having a stranger pay attention to her house. When she asked Frank if he wanted another beer, he said instead, "You'll have to calm down with all this stuff. It's getting out of control."

Darla enjoyed her collecting. She'd gotten started on ceramics at the suggestion of her daughter Arlene who now lived in Encino, California, with a man who sold motorcycles. Arlene said that a hobby was one of the best excuses to get out of the house. Although Darla didn't want to leave her house nearly as much as to have visitors come to it, she took her daughter's suggestion. But ten months after she'd begun the ceramics class, the shop closed. Darla would have had a forty-five-minute drive to the new location and, at the altered class time, run into all kinds of traffic. By then, she had become more interested in placing objects on her lawn than in painting and baking them, anyway. Completing an individual piece became less satisfying. What began to thrill her was the big picture—the accumulation displayed on her lawn.

Darla started sending for decorative items pictured in catalogs. Ordering became as routine as having pizza delivered. Yet even the simplest things were dangerous: on Wednesday Darla had seen a program on TV about pizza trucks getting into accidents as drivers hurried to deliver the pies hot. Whenever Darla tried to explain danger in the most familiar places to her younger daughter, Morna, the girl called Darla neurotic. Darla talked to Morna on the phone once a month. With her life in a constant state of flux—new jobs and boyfriends and apartments—Morna seldom called from the same place twice.

"That girl's something else," Darla would tell Frank and then cry, even though she was a little envious of Morna's devil-may-care attitude.

"Get the skunk if you want," Frank said to Darla, reaching for her hand. "How about another couple of beers for us, too?"

Frank's change of life had come earlier—when he was about forty—and then nothing had made sense. He hadn't wanted to collect things, only to get rid of any objects that identified him as a husband or a carpenter or a father. He had longed to be an outlaw, on the run with no possessions except a horse to take him wherever he got it in his mind to go. What he wanted then and what his family needed had pulled at him until he felt a physical stretching across his chest, a tightness.

Darla tried to stop fixating on the best location for the skunk. If she didn't concentrate on the game, Frank would see that she was still thinking of the catalog items. He could do that every once in a while. The other day, she'd seen a TV program featuring couples who had grown to look alike as they'd aged. Although the program host had specified diet as the major contributor to the phenomenon, Darla didn't think everything could be reduced to chemical reactions. With the exception of the lawn ornaments, she and Frank laughed at and scowled over pretty much the same things. It followed that similar lines had settled along their eyes and mouths. Darla's lines were a little more pronounced than Frank's because, in public, Frank seldom changed facial expressions dramatically. If she didn't color her hair a deep auburn shade, she and Frank would both be gray and even more of a match. Darla thought the program on people who resembled their pets had been much more interesting than the one on husbands and wives.

Although Frank and Darla had only heard one car squeal down Route 82 on Saturday night, on Sunday morning the position of Darla's leprechauns had been changed. One seemed to hold up the other's legs like kids in a wheelbarrow race. Frank assured Darla that the pose was meant to resemble a sex act.

"Get out," Darla said. But she hurried down the steps to right the statues.

"That's it. Fix them up before somebody sees them on the way to Mass," Frank said and had to laugh. "Let's go get a few rolls and doughnuts," he called. How could the woman he'd lived with for thirty-two years ignore certain facts: that the appearance of the front lawn said something about the people who lived inside the house; that once people started taking liberties with your possessions, there was sure to be more trouble.

At the bakery Frank selected their doughnuts, and Darla picked up the Sunday paper in the pharmacy next door. She spotted a tabloid with a headline about a doctor jump-starting a patient's heart with battery cables. The articles in that paper were crazy, but they never pressed at her the way the real news did. Datelines of riots and murder in faraway places made her worry that those spots were the very ones where her younger daughter could be. There was no telling where Morna's next card would be postmarked.

Frank saw Darla studying the tabloid and said, "If you don't watch it, our yard might find its way onto the front page."

Darla wondered if she really could inspire headlines with her lawn ornaments. Those papers always featured articles on people with an overabundance of one thing or another—times they'd kissed Elvis Presley, or children they'd had, or things they'd been addicted to, or days they could go without carbohydrates. If Darla were highlighted similarly, maybe the news would reach Arlene and Morna.

A strange car was parked in Frank and Darla's driveway when they arrived home.

"Who the hell's this?" Frank said. It wasn't even ten-thirty.

"Oh, hello," said a doughy woman with short, very curly blonde hair. She wore a red and white striped dress. As Frank and Darla stared at her, the woman said, "I see you haven't put prices on anything yet. I *am* a little early."

"What's she talking about?" Frank asked Darla.

"What are you talking about?" Darla asked the woman.

"Why, the tag sale," the woman said almost indignantly.

"What tag sale?" Frank and Darla both asked.

"The tag sale I saw in the paper."

"There's some mistake," Darla said, and she pulled the Sunday paper from her bag and searched through the classifieds.

"There," said the woman, pointing at the line ad.

Darla explained that the woman had gotten the wrong house. Thelma Boyd, their neighbor three houses down, was having the sale.

"I just figured," the woman said, looking around at the forest of ceramic and wood and plastic creatures. "I should have known," she said more confidentially to Darla. "I've never been first to one of these things in my life. And I've been hitting tag sales for nearly thirteen years."

Before Darla finished making a pot of coffee, Frank had tacked a sign to the mailbox—TAG SALE—with a bright red arrow pointing in the direction of the Boyd house.

The following week, before Frank got home from work, three women from the neighborhood appeared at the front door. Helen, Carol, and Ruth huddled together on the porch. Darla hadn't had visitors in so long that she wished the three had called ahead so that she could have gotten some chips and sherry, and made a little onion dip. But as soon as they were in the house, Darla realized the visit was not for a friendly chat; it was a mission.

Ruth, the tallest and youngest, spoke first. "We've come to talk to you about your yard." At the word "yard" all three women looked out Darla's front window, from which they could just see the hooves of the kicking donkey.

"What about it?"

"It's—it's—" Helen practically stuttered. Darla had known Helen for years. When their children were babies, Darla and Helen had compared progress on teething and toilet training. They'd talked over cups of coffee and glasses of wine. If Darla had to run to the store, Helen would watch Darla's kids on a moment's notice, and Darla did the same for Helen.

"Let's face it, it's overdone. You can't think *that* much stuff is attractive," Carol blurted. Darla had never really liked Carol. She and her husband were extremely cheap. At last year's IBM company picnic, the two had filled their party hats with jumbo shrimp from the buffet table and then stashed the seafood in a cooler in their car trunk.

"What business is it of yours?" Darla asked, looking directly at Carol and avoiding Helen's eyes.

"If you'd like some help," Ruth said.

"What help?"

"Some of the little things are cute," Helen said, touching Darla's arm. The children who'd originally drawn them together now pointed out the women's differences. Helen was a grandmother assured of the attention of some member of her family every weekend; Darla tended lifeless statues.

"A few are fine," Ruth said.

Darla felt trapped. They were asking her to choose from among her collection. Pick two or three. It was like selecting between her children. If she could have only one of her daughters come home and live within five miles of her, which would she choose? Arlene, living in California with a man Darla had never met, or the wandering Morna, who could be anywhere?

"This is my house. I'm not doing anything wrong," Darla said firmly.

"No one's accusing you of anything," Ruth said.

"We're just asking you if you wouldn't mind considering your neighbors is all," she went on. Ruth had very large, white teeth that appeared to snap at her words as she spoke.

"What authority do you have?" Darla asked Carol directly.

Ruth raised her hands in a gesture that appeared to be surrender. "We're the Neighborhood Beautification Committee," Ruth said and smiled at Helen and Carol.

"Since when?" asked Darla.

"Since now," Carol said, explaining how she had to look at Darla's "mess" every time she drove down the street to get onto 82.

"It might be different if you lived way at the other end of the street," Helen said softly.

As the women left, Darla watched them pointing to her assembly of decorations, which stood unaffected in the midst of controversy.

Darla paced around her house and wondered, why now? Maybe the grazing sheep had caught their attention and been the breaking point. More likely, they'd finally gotten the courage to approach her. Perhaps the entire twelve-house neighborhood had delegated the three women to call. All Darla's older neighbors had a slew of grandchildren; the younger ones gave monthly house parties. They filled their houses with children and friends and pets.

Darla hadn't realized how far she'd drifted away from her neighbors until last summer, when she'd planned a party. She had decided on a Mexican menu with taco salad and avocados and enchiladas. But when only two couples accepted the invitation, Frank said to let someone else give the parties. He promised the cases of Mexican beer wouldn't go to waste.

Blotting her eyes with a Kleenex, she looked out on her lawn. For a minute, each of the statues marked something that had been lost to her—daughters, grandchildren, a decent education, the shoes she couldn't afford for her senior prom, the sister who had died at birth, the pencil case that had been stolen from her on her first day of school. Her mother. And, along the way, her neighbors.

When Frank joined her in the kitchen and got out the spaghetti pot, Darla felt guilty for indulging in self-pity even for a moment.

"Linguine or ziti?" he asked.

All she needed, as Arlene had said, was a change of environment, Frank thought. "Get her out of the house," his daughter had advised. Frank would do that in January when he took his week's vacation. Normally, he spent that time doing repairs around the house, but this year they'd take off for Florida to see his father, or maybe Encino, where Arlene was working as a waitress. But Darla might need to vacation where no one knew her—Boston or Baltimore—so she could relax and look at new things without any interference from the past. Bernie had recommended Atlanta. If Darla went easy on the Christmas gifts this year, Frank thought he could swing the trip.

Frank was so thoughtful about cooking dinner that Darla almost told him of the neighborhood resistance to their lawn. But she didn't. It was like the time, twenty-eight years ago, when she'd suspected she was pregnant with Morna. Arlene wasn't a year old. She wasn't supposed to be pregnant again, not so soon, not when Frank was between jobs and they were just getting back their private time together. Darla hadn't told him because she'd hoped that if she didn't say anything, the baby would go away.

Only Morna hadn't gone away. The cause of Darla's anxiety became a baby, then a cranky child, then a girl and a young woman who never seemed content with where she was—not in school or in her own room at home. It was as if Darla's early regret at being pregnant had been absorbed by the child, who believed she'd never really been welcomed. And instead of assuring her younger sister a place in the family, Arlene had followed Morna's contrary directions. After hours of frantic searching or telephoning, Darla would come upon her daughters smoking under the bridge over Sprouss Creek, waiting for the Top Hat bus line in front of the convenience store, hitchhiking south on 82. Darla was never sure where they thought they were headed, just as now it was hard to picture exactly where they were.

Darla looked out at the figures, each with a specific place on the lawn. The Pattersons' Labrador was sniffing and weaving among them. Darla rapped on the window. The animal didn't notice Darla, or if he did, to spite her, he lifted his leg on the plastic cow. Darla ran out the side door and chased him off. Then she rinsed the cow with the garden hose.

"It's a dog," Frank said, trying to explain away Darla's distress by repeating the word "dog." "They do that anywhere."

Frank worried that Darla was getting a little too touchy about the leprechauns or whatever the hell it was the dog had pissed on. People were supposed to keep things *inside* their houses, not display their preferences in colors and sizes and shapes for the world to see. Things were safe, or at least safer, within your house, which you could lock, where you could keep possessions dry and private. Sometimes Frank thought his wife forgot the basics, the way things worked.

"You've got to expect things like this," Frank said.

Darla knew he was right, although it was hard for her to watch some old dog deliberately mark one of her lawn pieces. The sheep, the swans, the ducklings were so exposed, so naked outside the safe interior of her house. Still, she felt a need to know that the ornaments could hold up out there in spite of dogs and rain. And nosy neighbors. The figures were like a litmus test for tolerance.

While Frank went to the stove for seconds of linguine, Darla studied the knickknacks in the shadow box hanging on her living room wall. When Arlene was in high school, she'd spent all of her savings one Mother's Day on a tiny cup. It was the only thing she could afford by Goebel, the company that made Hummel figurines. Darla had always wanted a Hummel, but they'd been way beyond her budget. The day Arlene gave her the little china cup, Darla cried over the hand-painted scene of a forest and a baby carriage. She never told her daughter that the small cup was one you gave as a baby gift. Now she held the cup, then examined a leaf-shaped ashtray Morna had made in Girl Scouts, a handblown bud vase that had been her mother's, a set of salt and pepper shakers in the shape of a knife and spoon that Frank had brought her from Florida the time he'd moved his father there. She took the whole collection outside and placed each piece along the wrought-iron railings on the front porch. That would show those busybodies, Carol and Ruth.

Frank tried not to act surprised. "What's going on?" he asked. "Why don't you leave that and come have some coffee?"

"In a minute, Frank."

Frank saw that his wife was arranging the items as a display, not just dusting or airing them. "What the hell is going on?" he demanded.

Darla said, "Frank," stretching his firm, clipped name into syllables. Nobody came around to notice her mementos anymore. Nobody traded secrets or lingered over coffee in the living room with Darla's prized, fragile possessions sitting against the mirror of the shadow box. Did she force herself on people as Frank suggested, or were people afraid that her house, empty of children and grandchildren, was contagious?

"The next thing, you'll be setting the goddamn furniture on the lawn," Frank yelled. "Or you'll be finding a place for me out there with the rest of that crap."

"Frank," Darla said again. She tried to talk but no words came, only desperate hand motions and wetness in her eyes.

"Why don't you get that stuff in here and come out to the kitchen with me?" Frank said, going back inside. When he had first married Darla, she never came to bed without hiding herself in a thick, sweet-smelling nightgown. Now she put herself right out in the open, pushed her tastes on the world, pressed herself on people until they turned away.

"You want one of these?" he called, staring at the cold can of beer in his hand. Listening for her response, he heard the clinking of collectibles being replaced in the shadow box.

Later that night, Darla heard sounds. They were not dog noises or squealing cars, but hushed voices slipping through the three-inch opening of the bedroom window. Darla lay awake, stiff with fear. She smelled smoke and heard something crack. "Frank," she said, "do something."

Frank heard the noises, too. The kids again, preying on the

figures. "I'm not going out there," Frank said. Last week Bernie had been held up by two teenagers with Saturday night specials. "I didn't know they were actual guns, for Christ's sake," Bernie had said. "I thought they were water pistols. These things happen. You read about it all the time. Some poor goof getting robbed by kids with toys."

"So you were a hero," Bernie's wife had chimed in. She'd rolled her eyes at the word "hero" and pointed to Bernie's bandaged arm. A few minutes later, she'd turned serious and said how lucky they were.

Frank hoped he would be lucky tonight.

The noises grew louder, the clashing and crashing like the sounds of the cop shows on TV. Whispering became outright laughing. Frank had to admit he'd been expecting trouble, but nothing so frightening. Nothing that opening the front door and turning on the porch light wouldn't solve.

He peeked out the window and saw people moving across the lawn, a small fire and, replaced at some point on the porch railing, Darla's knickknacks pointing at the front door like arrows to Frank's vulnerability. As he picked up the telephone to call the police, Frank was shaking.

At the sound of sirens, the intruders ran off. In the swirling police lights, the figures Darla had made and collected resembled war casualties. Broken beaks and legs and arms and feet littered the dark lawn. In the place where the flamingo had stood was a flesh-colored melted mass. The neighbors looked on from a safe distance.

"You can't say I didn't warn you," Frank said, putting his arm around his wife. He felt her shaking, and he squeezed tighter to keep her in place and to hide his own uncertainty.

Darla hadn't seen all her neighbors together since the block party years earlier when the kids were babies. They'd all stood in place in the street, set styrofoam cups of beer and paper plates full of food on the roofs and hoods of their cars, and looked with satisfaction at their houses lined up along the street. Frank had said how glad he was to live in a real neighborhood with people you could count on. Now Darla bent into Frank and kept her eyes on the motionless men and women. She thought she heard their voices coaxing her to join them again. The whispers formed a haunting breeze in the black air.

Nocturne

$\mathcal{G}$ale said she didn't like the way things were beginning. Checking in two hours before departure, Gene and Gale were advised that their nonstop flight to St. Kitts had been cancelled. The night before, they'd driven to Brooklyn from their home in Springfield, Massachusetts, to spend the night with Gale's mother. There was a morning flight from Kennedy airport. Now the ticket agent was telling them they'd have to change planes in Puerto Rico.

"Somebody should have called you," the agent said.

"Why didn't somebody call us?" Gale echoed without really challenging the young man. Gene could see that his wife's usual pluck was tempered in anticipation of flying.

"If you hurry, I can get you on a flight that leaves in ten minutes," the agent said.

"This is just what I need," Gale said, running ahead of Gene. Her carry-on bag and pocketbook flapped against her new, loose-fitting, turquoise pants outfit. Her dark curls flew back from their usual soft frame around her face.

"It still beats the hell out of sitting in your mother's kitchen," Gene called back.

On the plane, Gale became uncharacteristically quiet and clung to Gene as if he were one of the flotation devices. He knew not to point out this comparison, not until they arrived in St. Kitts anyway. Maybe not until they touched down again in New York.

On land, Gale could deal with any predicament. In twenty-six years of marriage, she had put out a kitchen grease fire, set their oldest son's broken leg, held their twelve-year-old dog as it was put to sleep. She'd delivered twins—eight pounds each—in two hours and twenty minutes. And last year, during a teacher recognition dinner for the junior high where Gene taught, she'd performed the Heimlich maneuver on the principal. Gale could go into action before Gene's own adrenalin ever kicked in.

But in the air or on water, Gene took charge. That was one of the invaluable things they'd learned early, and it had spared them countless arguments. Not like Gene's sister and brother-in-law, who'd been married almost as long as he and Gale but still fought about who would go for the Sunday paper.

Gene and Gale had long ago worn smooth the initial rough spots. The only thing that bothered Gene these days was Gale's obsession with becoming a singer. At nearly fifty. At a good twenty pounds heavier than the day he'd met her.

They had a two-hour layover in San Juan. "I'll try to find us something to eat," Gene said.

"I can't eat," Gale said flatly. "But you go on ahead."

Gale waited at the gate for St. Kitts, while Gene went off to scout out a hamburger. When he returned with a package of corn chips, the huge windowed room was teeming with Spanish voices and smoke and more babies than Gene wanted to count. Sitting on the edge of her seat, Gale clung to their two pieces of luggage as if they were her children. He imagined she was playing a song in her head, something like "The Girl from Ipanema," which was one of her favorites. She told him once that just thinking of music helped calm her down.

"The flight's been delayed," she said breathlessly, though she didn't appear to have moved since he'd left her.

"Well, maybe I should warn the hotel," Gene said.

When he returned the second time, Gale was frantic. It didn't help when he told her he hadn't been able to get through to the hotel.

"Would you still take this over my mother's kitchen?" Gale asked.

He tried to entertain her by pointing out a heavyset man wearing a baseball cap backward and carrying a plastic bag filled with sandwiches. "Think he's our pilot?" He didn't get as big a laugh as he'd anticipated.

Despite Gale's anxiety over flying, she hadn't blamed Gene, hadn't said, "If we'd gone to Florida like *I* wanted, we wouldn't be here." Initially she'd mentioned Florida for his spring break. It wouldn't have been Gene's choice; still, for Gale's sake, he had been prepared to spend a week in Mickey Mouse territory. But Gene got nervous when she'd mentioned that if he took early retirement in a few years, and she quit her medical receptionist job, they could move to Florida, where she could supplement their income by singing.

When he'd pressed her with, "But why Florida?" she had given a lengthy answer, not totally satisfying. It involved both the mood evoked by the weather and the residents, who were generally older and probably would enjoy her renditions of old songs. It wasn't until he'd remembered that her parents had been planning to move to Florida before her father's Alzheimer's sucked their savings dry that Gene understood the connection.

He couldn't imagine living anywhere but New England, where he'd been born, where his ancestors had staked out their claim to the new land as innkeepers. So when he won a secondary Lotto price of $75,000, he selected the St. Kitts vacation package for the beaches and weather that his wife loved, and because it wasn't Florida.

"You think that's our plane?" Gale asked over the wails of a baby behind her. She pointed toward a prop plane that Gene guessed held about fifty seats. Gene shook his head no, just as an announcement was made to passengers en route to Antigua and St. Thomas. A third of the waiting room emptied. He suggested they go find a bar or some souvenir stand, but Gale said she was sure that as soon as she walked off with their bags the flight would be announced.

When the sun started to set, and oranges and reds filled the windows, Gene tried to think not about how Gale would handle flying in a small plane in the dark, but about her preoccupation with a singing career. She'd complained that their house was empty since their oldest son had married and the twins had gone off to college. Gene remembered Gale singing to the boys when they were babies—low, crooning lullabies—and how she'd tried to coax each of them into piano lessons, glee clubs, church choirs, even guitar lessons, all to no avail. He hoped that once she got used to life without the boys, her preoccupation with music would pass. But when she put something on her agenda, it was near impossible to dissuade her. He'd never heard her sing an entire song. He'd caught phrases, listened to her humming melodies along with the radio, but that wasn't enough for him to be sure of the quality of her voice.

Planes, progressively smaller, taxied in and out of the airport; announcements were made for flights to St. Martin and Trinidad and other islands Gene had never heard of. The waiting room emptied and refilled again and again while Gene and Gale stuck to their plastic chairs.

It was nine o'clock when the flight to St. Kitts was finally announced. With all the delays and cancellations, Gene figured a sizable crowd would board the plane. But besides Gene and Gale, there were only three other passengers—an elderly woman with a young boy who must have been her grandson, and a large man wearing an immense cowboy hat. Gene could feel Gale quaking. The five of them filed out into the warm dark air to a plane that looked as if it could accommodate a dozen passengers at most.

"It's a good thing we didn't check our bags," he teased. The other passengers' suitcases were pitched like giant basketballs into a netlike container attached to the outside of the plane.

"Oh my God," was all Gale said as Gene ushered her, head down, into the tiny cabin. Gene felt her fear invading him like a cold.

The pilot looked no older than some of Gene's students. Before the kid pulled the shower-curtain divider between the cockpit and the passengers, Gene caught a glimpse of the instrument panel decorated with stickers. "Panic button" caught his attention. There was also a Ninja turtle and a calendar featuring a flock of women in bikinis. He bent toward Gale, who stared at the propeller directly outside the window. As the plane bumped down the runway, he held her sweaty hand.

"It's only a couple of hours, Gale. You can handle this," Gene said. She didn't answer.

When the plane lifted gently into the blackness, swayed, held, then ascended, Gene wondered if the trip was a mistake. It was so far from his usual reference points of classrooms and cars and lawns that he thought, Maybe I'm dead. Maybe I had a heart attack the moment I discovered that I won the lottery. But as he settled into the plane's drone, and spotted the occasional lights of other islands and the moon turned on its side, he thought he heard Gale starting to hum. He turned to her just as she mumbled, "This is longer than any damn two hours."

Gene's tan corduroy jacket hung in the hotel closet; he had forgotten about the russet and gold colors back home and allowed the turquoise sea, the brilliant green, and flowering pinks of St. Kitts to soak into him. He was glad not to be standing in classrooms full of inattentive eighth and ninth graders, relieved not to hear his wife humming bits of old songs he couldn't remember. At times, he felt as if the sun were bleaching his mind to a pale version of itself, and that was a comfort. He forgot about Gale's remark that the difficult time they'd had reaching the island might be a sign of more trouble to come.

Gene hadn't gone through the crises that most of his fellow teachers agonized over. He hadn't bought a sports car or slept with a woman half his wife's age. His job was what he did; he got whole summers off, was at the top of his pay scale—and that would probably go up the next time the school board negotiated a contract.

His wife hadn't found aging nearly as acceptable. Gene's brother-in-law Bob had said, "Women don't lose their creative energy when the kids grow up." Bob confided that his wife had joined a group of women writers and was working on a book of poems. Somehow poetry sounded a lot safer to Gene than singing, especially forgotten songs that could be performed only in Florida.

Not that Gale had mentioned anything about singing since they'd left home. Gene hadn't even heard her in the shower. But he felt her ambition was still intact, like the off-shore cruise ship that would eventually spew a barrage of tourists onto the island. Gene would have opted to remain stretched out in the sandy heat day after day, creamed with SP15 sun protection. But by agreeing to Gale's daily activities, he felt he was staving off the larger issue of her music career.

Throughout the week, Gale led Gene to an array of restaurants and on shopping expeditions. The extra-large T-shirts she finally settled on looked huge, but she insisted they'd shrink. And just when Gene settled in the sun with a book, Gale wanted to gamble.

She loved the slot machines at Jack Tar Village. The extent of Gene's involvement was cashing in a hotel coupon that awarded him five dollars in quarters. Gale shook her head at what she called his New England upbringing; she said tightness was bred right into him.

"Why don't you put a few of those quarters in the slots?" Gale said.

"I've used up all my luck," he said, reminding her of the lottery win.

"Well, I sure haven't," she said, jerking the arm of the slot machine nearest her.

When the couple drove out beyond the hotel grounds, they found the distances between resorts awash with deteriorating buildings, broken roads, and children poking absently at the earth with sticks. The contrast between the sleek tourist accommodations and the disintegrating shacks was startling, as if the residents had been weathered, their pastels a soft echo of the brilliant hues around them. When he shared this theory with Gale, she said simply, "The sun must be getting to your brain," and kissed him softly on the forehead.

After dinner, just when he'd put aside his concern over her

singing ambitions, he found her in the doorway to the lounge staring at a sexy woman poised before a glossy piano.

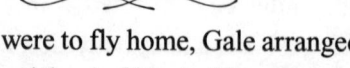

The day before they were to fly home, Gale arranged for a ferry trip to the neighboring island of Nevis. Throngs of native workers got off the boat Gene and Gale were about to board. An equally large crowd nudged him along the dock, and he let his body go limp as he moved forward, the brown and black arms and legs carrying him.

In the nine days since their arrival, Gene had gradually felt his will surrendering to the heat and the lassitude that seemed ancient, yet totally new. He'd begun to eat slower and walk slower. He had to make an effort to keep pace with his wife.

"If your hair was longer, she'd do it, too," Gale had said yesterday as she was having hers done in corn rows on the beach. He'd touched his fine, fair hair and looked up from his book now and then to watch the dark fingers working their way through his wife's shiny hair. He tried to imagine the reaction at the faculty meeting if he turned up with a dozen or more braids, each weighted with a brightly colored bead. The principal had gone crazy when Gene had let his hair grow to the top of his shirt collar. Gene had looked at his wife and tried to envision her fantasies. "Do you remember that song, 'Vamos a la playa'?" Gale had said to the gentle woman handling her hair.

The ferry trip was rough, and there weren't enough seats. Not until Gene led Gale up from the lower passenger area, arranged in long pews, and into the fresh air did she speak. "I've just about had it with this transportation from the dark ages," she said.

In Nevis the dock overflowed with cab drivers offering their services to the few tourists aboard the ferry. Gene and Gale passed by them and walked into Charlestown.

"Well, do you want to rent a car?" Gale asked.

"I think that's out of the question," Gene answered. The dusty, broken road curled through a congestion of old storefronts, few of them open, along the town's main street. The town, boasting no tourist accommodations or local handicrafts and souvenirs, appeared geared only toward the day-to-day needs of the islanders. Gene was fascinated with the simplicity, but Gale was a little testy.

"What the hell are we going to do all day until the ferry goes back to St. Kitts?" she asked. He could have said, "Hey, I thought this was *your* idea," but he just shook his head. After an early lunch and fifteen minutes in the only museum in sight—a tiny building dedicated to Alexander Hamilton—they made their way back to the drivers polishing their cabs in the sun.

The cab they selected for their tour of the island was an old Volkswagen van painted purple and yellow. The driver slid the door open, and the couple settled onto worn seats covered with layers of towels. Gene's trepidation turned to awe as the van rounded corner after corner of spectacular tropical scenery. Palm trees flared out against the different blues of the sky and ocean. Small shacks lining stretches of the waterfront appeared blanched like bone. Gene felt himself moving farther and farther away from the civilization he knew—painted and varnished and polyurethaned and weatherproofed and rust-proofed, second coated and undercoated. Here there seemed to be only the natural world and a few buildings taking a stand against it.

Some of the roads James, the driver, took were simply two parallel strips of concrete about a foot wide. He delivered Gene and Gale to a church, two graveyards, and an ancient mineral springs bathhouse before they stopped for a drink at an old sugar plantation, which had been converted into a resort. At the poolside bar Gene and Gale ordered drinks of native rum and Coke, and Gene bought James his drink of choice—a bright orange Fanta.

Traveling again, Gene watched the lush scenery as James rambled on, sending the stories of the island's history and its recent independence through the van. Gale looked attractive with her deep tan and fuchsia-colored dress. Gene, plastered with SP15, was as pale as the underbelly of a fish. The color of his short-sleeved shirt, advertised as "lemon" when he'd bought it a couple of years back, was practically white. Despite the fact that he always wore a hat, his hair had gotten lighter. Next to his wife, he felt as washed out as any of the dwellings they passed. The vacation that was supposed to make them forget about their differences was exaggerating them. All along he'd thought that he and Gale would want the same thing when they got older, especially a long Thanksgiving table overflowing with food and kids and grandkids. Now she'd rather be singing in cocktail lounges or gambling than wiping off tiny mouths.

By the time they made their final stop before the ferry, Gene was light-headed from a succession of rum and Cokes, and Gale was humming "Stormy Weather."

"What do you say? One more before we tackle the ferry back?" Gene asked Gale. She giggled and when she squeezed Gene's hand, he put his whole arm around her and pulled her in close. Maybe all she'd ever needed was a couple of drinks before boarding a plane or ferry to keep her enthusiasm intact. Maybe if he paid her more attention, she wouldn't feel so driven to sing.

The bar in the old building they entered was not as empty as the others had been. A stout but strong-looking man wearing a sleeveless T-shirt announcing "USA #1" stood in front of the bar area as if staking out a claim. Although the man didn't stop joking with two black men seated before him, Gene definitely felt scrutinized. Maybe by the blond man about his own age who leaned back on a bar stool, smoked a cigar, and stared at a mirror on the ceiling. Before Gene could get the money out of his pocket for a couple of drinks, the USA man ordered a round for the bar, still without looking directly at Gene or Gale.

USA #1 began telling a story, holding the attention of everyone at the bar. The silence that surrounded him reminded Gene of movies when someone was having a streak of luck at cards or craps. Held breaths and looks of awe adhered to the lucky one and momentarily made him physically bigger than he really was.

Suddenly, repeating words from USA #1's story, Gale said, "*I'm* from Brooklyn. Flatbush."

In a haze, Gene saw the man staring at Gale, drunk and probably feeling very far from home. The man extended his hand. He was deeply tanned, and curls of black and grey hair sprouted above the neckline of his shirt.

"Are you CIA?" the man asked without lowering his voice. His accent matched Gale's mother's. A couple of people at the other side of the bar laughed softly as if this were something the man asked routinely.

"What are you talking about?" Gene asked, wondering at once if the man mistook him for someone else.

The man introduced himself as Roy. Gale mentioned the names of a couple of people named Roy that she'd gone to high school with. Then she said, "Roys R Us," and laughed.

"You're not CIA?" Roy asked again.

"Do we look like we're from the CIA?" Gene asked. He felt both flattered and puzzled and, despite all the drinks, unsure of himself.

"How the hell do I know these days?" Roy said and smiled widely. Roy ordered another round, but Gene wasn't half finished with his first.

"Where do you suppose I could find a bathroom around here?" Gene said.

Roy pointed to a nearby row of palm trees and said, "I'll join you." Gene followed Roy, who seemed to know all the rules.

"What brings you here?" Roy asked as he unzipped in the bright sunlight. The faint breeze was the temperature of someone's breath.

"The ferry," Gene said. The men laughed over the hissing of their piss. "We're staying on St. Kitts. Vacation," Gene said.

"Vacation," Roy repeated. His voice was deep, reassuring.

"I won the lottery," Gene said proudly. He tilted his head back and looked deep into the canopy of palms. Gene realized that Roy was the first American he'd spoken to since he and Gale had left home.

"I want to show you something," Roy said suddenly, leading the way back to the bar. Authority was so tightly woven into Roy's persona that Gene felt uncharacteristically trusting of the stranger. "How long are you here for?"

"We go home tomorrow morning."

"Tomorrow," Roy said, then went quiet.

"He says it's time to go." Gale had appeared, gesturing toward James, the driver. "We don't want to miss the ferry."

Roy handed James some money, put his arms around Gene and Gale, and said, "I'll take you back." He pointed toward powerboats bobbing off a dock. "I'll show you St. Kitts like you've never seen it before."

"Great," said Gale. If Gene felt a twinge of uneasiness that Gale's practical plans for packing, enjoying a quiet dinner, and then writing last-minute postcards were cancelled, he was consoled when Roy said, "Just relax." Gene's father had said those words so often they were like his middle name.

Roy handled the powerboat with reckless competence, now and then catching a wave head on and sending the boat up in the air, then smacking back down again. Gale held onto Gene and squeezed him when they hit a roller. Her squeals made Gene think that she was enjoying herself. He licked his lips and tasted salt. "This is kinda fun," Gene said as the gulls just overhead turned back toward the dark form of Nevis.

"What?" Gale hollered above the boat motor.

Back on St. Kitts, Roy said, "Follow me." Gene was about to suggest that he and Gale return to the hotel, since they had a long travel day the next morning. But Gale was walking ahead, following close behind Roy, stumbling now and then on pieces of loose concrete.

Roy said, "Come on, Gene. Would you mind driving the Suzuki back to my house?" Before Gene could consider the situation, Roy directed Gale into a Lincoln. "Just follow me," Roy called.

Gene's heart pumped hard. Roy beeped his horn occasionally at oncoming cars and gave a generous wave out the window. All Gene held in his mind was keeping up. He didn't know what direction they were headed or notice the street names. When Gale turned around and waved at him, he felt like a kid pursuing a woman he knew nothing about.

They turned off a main road and drove along a dirt lane lined with sugarcane. When they came to a residential street, they began a sharp climb. Roy gestured, and, checking the mirrors, Gene saw the huge orange sun immersed in brilliant layers of red and purple and blue. As Roy continued to ascend, the land below them darkened and the water divided into separate bodies—the Caribbean Sea and the Atlantic Ocean. Distant silhouettes were islands. Gene was climbing to the top of the world. From this height, the local shacks and the children and chickens became less and less real. He stared at the sun falling farther and deeper into seawater. In his entire life he'd never seen anything so beautiful.

They stopped in front of an immense house that looked like a museum. "An architect from Greenwich Village designed it," Roy called proudly.

Gene felt sweat soaking his shirt as he accepted Roy's offer of a beer. With his free hand, Gene reached for Gale. "You'd better take it easy," he said quietly to Gale when she took a beer for herself.

"What do you think of this layout?" Roy asked proudly, showing them into a room featuring a long mahogany table and twelve chairs. A dark wooden candelabra hung from the ceiling. Outside, three Dobermans circled the pool. Gene thought he'd stepped onto a movie set without any idea of the role he was to play.

"He reminds me of someone," Gale whispered to Gene.

"I know everything that goes on," Roy said and laughed. He pointed out the window toward the airport. "I see what comes in and goes out." Thinking of the morning flight, Gene gulped audibly and nursed his beer.

Roy ushered them into the living room and introduced them to Johnny, the blond man they'd seen at the bar in Nevis. He was tall and walked slowly, with determination.

"This is Johnny," Roy said and laughed. "He runs the casino." Johnny pointed to a brightly lit complex well below them where Gale had won about ninety dollars. From where they stood, the ordinary collection of lights resembled a constellation.

Gene sighed with amazement at the spacious room, its ecru leather couches and huge modern paintings. Roy pulled Gene aside. What he said next made sense of everything. Roy thought the lottery win had made them millionaires.

Roy proposed that if Gene were to give him a minimum of $100,000, he could double the money in ten days. "You don't have to see anything. You don't have to know anything. You just give me the money. I can get you anything you want for yourselves," Roy offered. "Whatever you're into."

Gene wanted to say that all he was into was one beer at night before dinner. But he felt over his head talking to the man who, every once in a while, reminded him of his dead father.

"You could watch that sunset every night," Roy said and gestured at one of the floor-to-ceiling windows. Roy's offer for Gene and Gale to become his neighbors seemed genuine. Roy discussed the going rate for real estate. Gene ignored the numbers and fantasized about living at this perspective, where every mundane or impoverished detail appeared to be some kind of gem.

"I've got someone I want you to meet," Roy said. Gene and Gale followed as Johnny led them outside, beyond the Olympic-size pool, to a tiny cage.

"Percy," said Johnny.

Percy was a spider monkey. He cocked his head at Gene and Gale.

"This really gets him going," Johnny said, shaking a worn cloth doll at the monkey.

Percy screamed, jumped against the side of the cage, and

fell to the cage floor, screeching all the while, and then repeated the whole routine. Staring at the trapped animal, Gene discovered himself taking deep breaths.

"Stop," Gale finally said. "The poor monkey."

"You know how many monkeys I've killed?" Johnny said.

"Don't tell me," Gale said.

"Their hands make great back scratchers," the man said matter-of-factly.

Gale held tightly to Gene's arm the way she had in the plane from Puerto Rico. Gene thought it must have been months ago that he'd watched the waiting room in Puerto Rico filling and emptying and refilling as if breathing for some much larger body.

The four returned to the pale leather sofas. "What do you think? Isn't this paradise?" Roy asked softly. When neither Gale nor Gene answered, he asked, "What more could you want?"

"I could have an audience," Gale said, and Gene knew at once that when she'd been driving with Roy, she'd shared her ambition.

"So sing." Roy said the words that Gene never had.

Below them, hundreds of lights sparkled. Gale hesitantly began to sing "Moonlight in Vermont." Gene studied his wife, torn between feeling betrayed that she'd confided in Roy and touched that she was making the effort to ease their awkward dilemma.

As she gained confidence, Gale began singing louder, with passion, not at all like she'd crooned the lullabies for their tired babies. She stared directly at Gene as if she were performing for him alone. Her thin, untaught voice entered him, giving him courage. And when she finished, before the others could utter a word of praise or criticism, Gene clapped.